Goodbye from the Edge of Never

Goodbye from the Edge of Never

Steven Mix

Published by Falkor Publishing,
an Auryn Creative imprint.
www.falkorpublishing.com

Edited by Red Adept
Cover illustration by Ross Matteson
Cover design and book internal design by Auryn Creative
Character illustrations by Michael Merritt-Hutchins
Author photograph by P.I.C. Photo

ISBN 978-0-9896845-1-4
First Edition

www.stevenmix.com

ACKNOWLEDGEMENTS

Thank you to my friends and family for all their support. Big thank you to Mr. Kelly Reed and Mrs. Lynn McNamee from Red Adept. Huge thank you to Chris Garcia, Gerald Whalen and Carlos Moreno for being better men than I. A beautiful thank you to Christina Re and Shannon Somers from P.I.C. Photo for their gorgeous author photos. A very lyrical thank you to DOOMTREE for creating anthems to which I defy the undead. Finally, the most loving thank you is reserved for my wife. Her support allows me to create worlds.

-Steven

There's so much weird stuff related to the origin of this story. I had nine concussions in the army. Nine concussions; a damaged left frontal lobe; a damaged brain stem, back, and neck; two messed-up knees; and an injured ankle that pops with every step, all from a five-year enlistment in the army.

After my final concussion, strange things started to occur. The first month and a half was a blur. I was placed on quarters (meaning, you have to stay in the barracks to heal), and other paratroopers whom I outranked claimed I began to do strange things like waking them up and screaming about sweeping the floor four or five times in a night on Fridays and Saturdays between 3:00 and 4:00 a.m.

This wouldn't be a strange occurrence because the army plays games like this, but usually I was holding random items I did not realize I was holding while screaming at them. "I have no issues doing this, Specialist," one private said, "but you do realize you've asked us to do this three times already tonight, and why the hell are you holding a CD and a fistful of golf tees in your left hand?" My roommate at the time found me placing DVDs in the microwave. I was completely out of my head. I had undiagnosed whiplash for months, so my spine was stacked, causing me weird coordination issues with my left leg: I would drag it off to the side as I strolled along. It looked like an old-school zombie shuffle.

I would find out some time later, that a few individuals with traumatic brain injuries get weird obsessions. I don't know if it came from the movies I was watching or the leg shuffling, but I became obsessed with zombie pop culture, completely and utterly obsessed. Books, film, games—I even created a group in an online virtual community called the "Zombie Civil Rights Group," who not only became close friends who were equally obsessed with zombies, but also became a support group that would call and check up on my health while I was transferred over to the Warrior Transition Battalion for my injuries.

Every soldier in this war has nightmares. I had lost a really close friend, whom one of the characters from my story is named after. It is also the name I chose for my son when he was born, after the story was written. Losing my friend gave me an abnormal (or normal—hell if I know) amount of survivor's guilt. The nightmares you have from the service can be beaten back through the use of Ambien. What a great drug Ambien is. It not only helps you sleep, but it essentially stops you from dreaming most of the time. Does that sound awful, not dreaming? It's not if you have nightmares often. I have run out of Ambien a few times and, while awaiting a prescription refill, had the usual nightmares. Almost a year to the day after I had been discharged from the army, my nightmares changed from military themes to surreal amounts of darkness and suspense. Mason's backstory came from a nightmare that frightened me but wound up ending with a new day. One day after Mason's dream came Ashley's backstory. Donathan's backstory arrived a day after that. The only thing about these stories was they weren't quite about traditional zombies. The undead were dreamlike things that had mutated and changed.

The zombie community generally feels that there are two schools of thought on the undead: Traditional and New zombies. Traditional zombies are slow-moving and attack in mass numbers. New pop culture undead can run and do things that to some fans seem less zombie-like. Huge arguments erupt over fast movers vs. slow movers, whether zombies can originate from disease or magic, and what creatures can still be classified as zombies, etc. I don't want to get into it here, but this awesome community of people has some pretty phenomenal arguments.

If I was going to tell my story based on dreamlike versions of zombies, I had to step out from both schools of thought and just run with it. I broke some pretty cardinal rules and hoped that people wouldn't hate me for it. In books, there's often a rule that you never use the word "zombie" to describe the undead; you say anything else. However, we have seen in the real world, through that incident in Florida where a man high on the drug "bath salts" ate part of another man's face, that the whole world was just aching to scream the word "zombie." So, fuck that rule.

Even with my injuries, I was completely blessed. I had memory issues and some cognitive problems, but my intelligence was intact. As long as I wrote things down and was extra careful in stepping them through, I could conquer my adversity pretty well. Becoming a writer was something I had always dreamed of doing, and now it seems as though fate has just thrown me onto that path out of necessity.

While I was in the midst of creating the story and devising characters, Hunter S. Thompson died. One of my life goals had been to meet him, so I had to scratch that off my list and mourn his passing. It really bothered me that someone so entertaining wasn't walking under the same skies as me anymore, so I had to find a place for him in my book—well, Hunter S. Thompson as a character, anyway. In a lot of his writing, he would reference edges—the general idea that in order for people to be creative and to live more, they had to come close to one. One day, after pacing for hours in front of a community college, the title of the story just appeared before me, and I dropped my phone as I flipped out while trying to make a note of it. That's how I know something is great. If I panic and screw something up while I try to make a note of it, it's great.

Then I threw in everything that entertains me: comedic one-liners I've said, pop culture references; characters inspired by close friends (often based on what I thought their children would be like); comedy, fear, and as much action as possible; everything that entertained me or inspired me; my dreams, my nightmares, and the spaces between. They all went into the story. When it was written, I hoped it wasn't so insane that people would refuse to read it. Part of me still worries that too many people will read it, and I'll have to answer questions about my insanity. You might be able to spot which characters were inspired by different pop culture phenomena, and you'll definitely see tons of that in my story. I hope you enjoy it and are ready for the other books that will follow this one.

Sing, O goddess, the anger of artists, children of friends, that brought countless ills upon...
the zombies.

A gunslinger, a swordswoman, and an artist stood
on the edge of never, fighting back the darkness and
searching for a princess that time had long forgotten.

Music their shield and action their sword. Through the
melody of words yet unformed, they let the beat come
in.

But the darkness grinned back, for it had tricks too.
It changed, it snarled, it clacked it's teeth, and once or
twice it grew.

Tendons ripped and flesh ruptured as the darkness ran
screaming through.

1.

Rift Parish
Dan
Present Day

DAN REACHED DOWN and slapped dust off his faded dungarees, then took a pinch of tobacco and stuffed it into his lower lip. The day felt as though it had been one of the longest days of the year—too many tedious activities and not enough excitement. There had been no travelers over the last couple of weeks. He was starting to get concerned that maybe the word was out about the enclave, and they had received a reputation for the sacrifices they had to make. No one liked sacrifice, but his family sure seemed to enjoy the luxury that it allotted them.

Enclaves were the work compounds tied to most towns. Depending on the type of work they performed, they were often a ways off from everything else. Their work demanded they be about as far as one could get from a town and still support it economically.

He hadn't seen his family for two weeks, and that suited him just fine. When in town, he'd often be down at the local bar, drinking into the late hours just to avoid dealing with his kin. His kids were always harping on him and asking him thousands of questions about things that didn't matter, how the world once was or the meaning of this or that. Why should he have to answer that nonsense? He practically ran the town, and he certainly ran the enclave, at least since his father had passed away.

His dad had been too easy on people. He hadn't had the heart to make the tough decisions that would keep the town fed and the people warm. Demand respect, show you deserve it, and keep your people happy. The rest of the world could burn for all he cared. The rest of the world already had.

Twenty years ago, the first zombies had attacked towns, neighborhoods, and whole cities. It seemed the bigger the population, the greater the suffering. Safety in numbers wasn't quite the rule when the world was unprepared for something they thought was nothing more than fiction. Most of the populated parts of the world fell into ruin, and the survivors banded together to form towns and enclaves. All computer networks disintegrated in the first year of the attack while the digital age seemed to fade away. Some technology still worked, but people certainly weren't inventing new things. Most of the scientists left were experimenting on the undead to see if they could find a solution and save mankind. It was a fool's errand, but it kept his enclave in business.

Their trade was zombies—boarded up and shipped out alive. Well, sort of alive. They sent the zombies down various trade routes to science enclaves that would use them as guinea pigs, testing various concoctions that might save mankind. The business was profitable even if he didn't know where or how the scientists got their coin. He didn't care. His enclave was one of the biggest harvester operations on the west coast.

Taking stock of the shelves and aisles, he realized their food supplies were starting to get low. Originally, the place had been a hardware store where one could find "anything you wanted or needed for home and home repair." For his town, it was just a mass of items collected from travelers or scavenged from the ruins around them. Oversized shelves lined aisles two stories high, forming a maze of dusty relics from a civilization almost gone. At least the place funded his town well enough. If you had food on the table and your children weren't dying of thirst, you remained pretty well off.

"Jackson, c'mere," he called.

A tanned, balding man wearing a faded prison jumper, Jackson was trustworthy enough, probably because he feared Dan a bit. That was a good thing.

"I need you to head to Falling Sands and get us our supplies for the next month. Take three guys but make sure whoever you leave is good enough that they won't fall asleep on tower guard."

Jackson mumbled, "Yes, boss," and ran off.

Dan sometimes wondered if Jackson had some developmental issues or if he was just broken mentally by the general state of affairs. Most everyone was in some way. Once Jackson was gone, Dan became aware of a distinctive rhythm that seemed to echo off the cold, cement floors.

Gunfire erupted from above. That had to be the towers. Most of the roaming corpses didn't get very active until after about nine o'clock. The sun had only gone down an hour ago, but it wasn't terribly uncommon for a few stragglers to roam too close to the enclave at dusk. Still, that was a lot of gunfire for this hour. At least three towers must be going off.

In response to the gunfire, loud, hideous noises erupted from the collection of undead tenants in the caged-off sections of the compound. Poisoners retched, Shats hissed, and Ravens screeched as if the walls were falling. From where he stood, he could see a flurry of movement in the semi-dark aisles caged off from the rest by many layers of chain-link fence.

He looked up at the ceiling as if he could somehow see through sheet metal, scaffolding, and steel beams. "Someone tell those idiots to quit wasting so much ammo right after sundown!" Acting as though they'd never seen a zombie before was goddamned foolish.

More shots echoed, followed by shouting. Those couldn't possibly be zombies; they were armed. He'd heard of hunters attacking enclaves out of desperation, but it had never happened there. Rift Parish was part of the Shytown conglomerate on the Falling Sands trade route and was always armed to the teeth.

A loud explosion ripped through the enclave's south side. The entire building shook. A few shelves gave way behind him. Luckily, the blast wasn't anywhere near the zombie pens, but he still barked orders for men to go over and check them. He left the warehouse and hurried over toward the front of the compound. His feet slapped the pavement as he locked into a dead sprint, drawing his sidearm and cursing himself for not having a rifle with him. If the intruders were hunters, he could try to reason with them. Most didn't want to kill people; they just got paid for whatever zombies they put down. The big payoffs were nests found somewhere in the dead world, but a much easier bounty was sometimes to be gained by hitting the small harvester enclaves, killing whatever zombie population they had, dragging off the corpses to a faked nest, and getting paid. It was a dirty tactic that no one wanted to admit doing because people would kill you for messing with a trade route, but it did happen. The attackers would probably die outside the fence, but if not, he could always reason with them and pay them off.

He rounded the corner of one of the aisles and realized the source of the rhythm he'd been hearing. An old pickup truck had rammed into the compound, tearing a large hole into one of its walls before smashing into a stack of crates and coming to rest. Two oversize speakers were strapped in the bed of the truck, which extended higher than the actual cab. Loud hip-hop beats were blasting from them. He couldn't see anyone in the cab, so the people must have rigged it to drive into the wall on its own. Dan didn't recognize the song and really didn't care at that point. Ducking behind the cover of an ancient cash register hutch, he saw three small silhouettes emerge from the breach and begin firing on the guards inside the warehouse.

They moved with a swiftness and determination that suggested military training. As one loped into the room in one direction, the others rushed in the other direction until they were lined up behind cover and pushing forward at alternate moments. Dan's men couldn't seem to get a bead on them. After a moment, he realized they seemed to use the music to cue their movements. The way they avoided gunfire was almost mystical. The one on the far right seemed to be firing the most but moving the least. He didn't seem to care very much about hitting anyone, either. He was throwing down a wall of lead just to keep the guards suppressed as the other attackers moved. He only seemed to move when he absolutely had to, avoiding one of the guards who tried to flank him on the other side of an aisle. Rounds whizzed past, and Dan fell to the concrete as the old wood from the hutch shattered, raining splinters down on him. He was certain only a minute had passed, but it seemed like an eternity since the gunfight had begun. Finally, he peeked out from behind what was left of the hutch.

The shadow on the far left had moved quite a ways forward. There was just enough light there to see the person. It was a small Asian girl who couldn't have been much older than 25, crouching behind a mass of old steel wheelbarrows and using them as cover from what little gunfire Dan's men were able to retaliate with. She wore a sleeveless white tank top with a strap over it, crossing front to back, a skirt that seemed to blend black with purple, and a pair of old black Converse sneakers.

She shifted out from behind her cover as one of the guards appeared out of an aisle and rushed toward her with a shotgun. For a moment, it looked as though the guard had the upper hand. She threw down her rifle then quickly sprinted toward him. As the guard stopped running to gain his footing and raise his gun to fire, she fell backward into a perfect straight-leg slide as any seasoned baseball player might. Her back was almost flat, one foot pointed and her other leg bent underneath. She slid right between the guard's legs and reached up to clutch the buttstock of his shotgun. Her momentum carried her past as she successfully tore the gun from his grasp. Once she coasted away from him, she leaped to her knee and spun around, firing one round of ammunition into the guard. The man became a crumpled mess on the floor. The bass-filled music crescendoed as she raised the shotgun like an axe over her head and heaved it across the clearing while charging out of sight to find more cover.

That tiny woman just ran into a gunfight without a weapon!

For a split second, the sidearm felt heavy in his hand as Dan realized he hadn't taken a shot. There was little chance his rounds would have connected at this distance anyway. At least he'd be safe for a minute behind the hutch.

The music picked up again as something in the middle of the clearing shifted, surged forward, and caught the falling shotgun. It seemed blurry and out of focus for a moment until Dan realized it was just moving too fast for his eyes. Halting a moment to fire the remaining round from the shotgun, a man finally appeared where the blur was. He was taller than the other two and had slightly curly, dark-brown hair and a face that almost seemed chiseled from stone. The look he wore was a strange half smile crossed with determination. He was wearing a tan leather duster, jeans, and a pair of cowboy boots. With his look, this man could've easily been a gunslinger from the Wild West; the only thing missing was a cowboy hat. After he fired the remaining round, he shoved the shotgun into a guard who was rushing forward. He then threw back the side of his duster and drew a pistol with his left hand. He fired two more rounds with lightning speed and surged forward again.

As he disappeared from sight, another guard ran up, turned toward the gunslinger's back, and raised his rifle. The guard gasped as he was knocked off his feet and sent skittering across the room by the third shadow, who had run forward from his position and smashed into the guard with the force of a freight train.

This man seemed less trained, more clumsy. His looks were so shocking Dan had to do a double take. Standing at about six feet, the man was skinny and wearing an old desert-camo bulletproof vest, brown cargo pants, and striped sneakers. He also wore a hockey mask painted with an ominous red, black, and yellow picture.

The man himself seemed disproportionate. Although he was lean, his pockets bulged almost to bursting. Under his left shoulder hung a full-size machine gun, which he fired from his hip as he trotted forward to cover.

Once the thin man was out of sight, Dan decided he'd had enough. He was going to get the drop on at least one of them or die trying.

Sprinting around the corner, he was greeted by a sobering sight. What was left of his men had surrendered, raising their hands while backing away from their weapons on the floor. He lowered his pistol and let it clatter to the floor as the gunslinger motioned for him to join the rest of the group. They were then directed to a sectioned-off part of the building as the girl and the man with the hockey mask ran off, presumably to clear the rest of the building. The music from the truck finally stopped.

Twenty minutes passed, and the popping of shots died down. The wall creaked as the truck on the far side was moved to block the hole it had created. The gunslinger never flinched. His eyes rested on the group with a stern stare, but he still maintained his half smile. The only time it ever wavered was when one of Dan's men tried to speak. The gunslinger firmly told him, "Shut up."

The two others rejoined the gunslinger, and Dan noticed the girl had a baseball bat tucked into the holster on her back. Instead of talking, they made hand gestures and used sign language. Since the man wearing the hockey mask was back, Dan could see that the picture painted on his mask was a blond boy's face. The painting's statuesque features were highlighted by a red and black background. It looked like an old soviet propaganda poster.

The gunslinger seemed to be able to read what the others were signing without actually looking at their gestures. He never took his eyes off the members of the enclave.

Finally, the gunslinger said out loud, "That's fine. We'll kill all of the zombies."

So that was their game, Dan thought. They were hunters after all, just here to make a quick buck. Seizing the opportunity, Dan tried to reason with them. "If it's money you're after, we can pay you," he said harshly.

The gunslinger smiled even more then, wedging his pistol in his belt as he produced a second pistol from the right side of his coat, unlocked the magazine, and began reloading it. "Tell me more," he said in an amused tone.

Sensing that he wasn't being taken seriously, Dan added, "I promise you as much coin as you can carry, and you all can drag off any zombies you want."

The gunslinger just kept nodding and placing more rounds slowly into his pistol's magazine. When he finally finished reloading, he slapped the magazine back into the pistol and let the slide ease forward, chambering a round. Still smiling and nodding as he tugged the second pistol from his belt, the gunslinger slowly raised them both to aim at Dan.

Dan's promises trailed off as he realized the girl had a newly acquired rifle aimed at him, and the masked man was also pointing his machine gun in Dan's direction.

After drawing a tense breath, Dan groaned. "But wait... I'm not a zombie."

"We know," said the man behind the hockey mask.

The man then lifted his mask to reveal shaggy blond hair and a piercing gaze. Dan's eyes focused, recognizing the person, as all four weapons fired.

2.

New York

Taw...Taw...?

20 Years Earlier

TAP, TAP, TAP. The tips of his fingers made a hollow knocking sound against the plastered wall of the apartment.

Tap, tap, came the response.

Tap, tap, tap.

Tap.

A woman stood framed on both sides by large brick walls. "Jason, what are you doing?" she called.

"I was playing with my ball, Mom, but then I realized this wall knocks back... so now I'm just sort of playing a game with it," said the young boy with red hair and freckles.

"You shouldn't be doing that. Besides, we have to go meet your dad for breakfast."

Annoyed, the boy gave the wall one last tap as he turned to run back down the alleyway toward his mom's silhouette. The sun had just risen, causing all the shadows in the alley to stretch thin.

On the other side of the wall stood a man named... a man named...

What's my name? Taw... Taw... It was just here, I swear. Todd stumbled forward and backward and spun around. He'd clearly had too much alcohol or drugs or bad pizza. Something was wrong. His stained concert t-shirt was drenched in sweat, and his forehead felt both painful and on fire. He stood still for a moment, then he let his head sway, and his body followed suit forward, out the front door of his apartment and down the stairs. The sunrise felt... painful. There was too much noise from... somewhere. Todd's vision wouldn't clear, and he was having trouble blinking.

Rhythmic music carried down the street from a white sedan's stereo as it weaved up and down the city streets nearby. Todd slowly swayed back and forth for a minute before stumbling forward across the street. A red brick building nearby had a sign on it that read Orthodontist and had a phone number and a graphic of two small kids sitting next to each other, playing with blocks. Todd couldn't remember what an orthodontist was.

Something smelled fantastic. It was like strawberries, hamburgers, lilacs, and a sunny day all rolled into one. *Where is this coming from?* Finally, he realized a hot dog vendor was standing near him. The smell washed over him, and he was lost for a moment, trying to figure out what to do. His mouth was watering, and his mind screamed gibberish. Finally, he took a steady step forward with his eyes and hunger focused on the vendor.

The vendor, who had been looking the other way while setting up his stand, didn't notice Todd walking toward him. He reached down, picked something up, and unfolded it with a snap.

In an instant, Todd's view was blocked by the canopy of a rainbow umbrella. The sudden shock of this new object appearing in his way caused Todd to gasp and stumble backward. Instinctively catching the direction of his new momentum, he spun on one of his heels and faltered forward down the street away from the vendor.

The white sedan's loud music rattled windows as it drove past.

Todd's shoulders hunched forward a bit to keep up with his feet as he fumbled along. The memory of that scent lingered in his mind. It had smelled so delicious and felt so right, just thinking about it made his mouth and his eyes water.

As if answering his thoughts, the scent reappeared. This time, it came from an apartment to his left. Todd tried to stop but missed a step, tumbling forward for a second before managing to get his other foot under himself. The sudden sensation of tripping caused him to forget why he was there. He stood facing the doorway, wobbling left and right for a few moments. Finally, the scent caught his attention again, and he dragged himself forward.

Spotted brown linoleum greeted him as he crossed the apartment's threshold. The light was dimmer here, and everything felt cooler. An air conditioner was humming in the corner of the kitchen.

Todd's mind screamed, *Where's-a-scent?* as he shoved himself forward into the next room. His feet made dull, muffled thuds on the green shag carpet there. Next to an open screen door, an old tube TV played a tune that seemed familiar, as if he'd heard it playing a moment before from a car stereo. Todd felt lost for a second as he tried to focus his eyes on the television and think about the tune. The scent caught his nose again, and he turned slightly to his right to see an old woman sitting on a brown leather couch behind two TV trays, both with microwavable meals on them.

"Damned pervert," said a man behind him as a cane smashed Todd in the right side of his face.

The momentum caused Todd to stumble forward a few steps and smash out of the screen door, back onto the street. He stood for a moment in the morning sun, trying to figure out why his face stung a little. Nothing seemed to make much sense.

Tilting his head down, he lurched forward and let his feet shift down the street toward a busy intersection. Cars sped past Todd's left side as he neared it. He could see a group of people moving on the other side of the street and felt their excitement. It seemed to pulse off of them. Letting his body tremble for a second, he stood, trying to hear the sound of their words. The smell reappeared and surrounded him, leading him toward the people. A middle-aged couple talked to each other in excited tones as children standing nearby threw a ball to one another. Right in the very center of this group stood a beat-up red barbecue with kabobs sizzling on the grill.

That was enough to push Todd off the curb. His right foot stomped forward as his left dragged behind it. He just wanted to be close to that smell, to touch the source, to taste its pulse. He just had to—

A white sedan screeched to a halt on Todd's right as the driver laid on the horn. Todd spun away from it and fell forward onto his hands as the shrill horn continued on. When it stopped and Todd climbed back to his feet, the loud rhythm and beat could again be heard. Todd turned back to grunt his frustration at the driver before stumbling across the busy street into traffic.

Another horn sounded as Todd rushed past a truck. Tires screeched on his right. Once he passed the center lane, a blue compact skidded around him into a yellow Smart car. People shouted obscenities and frustration as they flew past him.

Once on the sidewalk, Todd noticed a small green flowerpot perched in the window of a yellow apartment with a matching green doorframe. Next to the flowerpot was an old square FM-band radio. Its antenna bent slightly near the end. Todd didn't even notice the song this time. He was too preoccupied with the smell urging him forward into the dark alleyway next to the apartment. The world around him shook as each step brought him closer to the source. His whole body felt stiff. His neck refused to stretch at the shoulder, and his leg continued to drag behind him as he shambled onward, desperately seeking his delicious salvation.

Trash littered the alleyway around a small gray dumpster with its hatches popped open. Although cold, the alley was dark, so it felt much more comfortable as Todd led off with his right foot and continued to let his left foot half-step behind. The tendons in his arms felt like steel girders that refused to bend at his sides as his head bobbed forward on his stiff neck. His breath rasped as he edged past the dumpster and halted at once.

It was here; the smell was right here next to him. Slowly, so as not to lose the scent, he began the process of shifting his swollen and stiff joints toward the scent on his right. Every second he moved caused him to hiss out a low, guttural noise. Finally, when he had turned far enough, his blurry vision rested on a transient who had stringy long brown hair and wore tattered rags and dark, stained blue jeans. The dark circles under the man's eyes seemed to reinforce the apathy with which he stared back at Todd. After a moment, the man lifted a large bottle of malt liquor from his side and took a long swig of it before pausing and pulling it forward just far enough to say with slurred words, "Whath the fuhck do you want?"

All at once, Todd's muscles came back to life as he lunged forward, snapping his jaws down on the man's face.

The world had been thrown into disarray. Most things were destroyed while a select few things almost seemed stuck in a time warp. Armageddon made life terrible, but it didn't seem to stop people from wanting to live. Once mankind had a taste for the good life, all they could do was try to emulate it while talking about how great life had been before the undead. Most of the world lost communication. North America was the first to fall victim, and everyone else soon followed. The world's economy had collapsed almost immediately when news of an "unknown plague affecting the recently deceased" was announced. No one wanted to put faith in any form of currency that wasn't tangible when one's grandmother, who had been dead for five years, could show up tomorrow and chew one's face off. Shortly after the announcement, most of the Internet went down, and for the first time in half a century, man had to start trying to rely on old communication systems and line of sight for messages. That pretty much signaled the end for most people. Living man turned on himself while dead men fed on the living.

Scientists around the world had been hard at work trying to figure out what made the dead rise. Although most referred to the dead as a plague, no nation ever announced a confirmation that the plague was caused by a virus or a disease. It never affected animals on a grand scale, so no one understood what it was exactly. Many scientists reasoned that it could have been a weapon developed by America's enemies, and it had grown out of hand when unleashed. Some even claimed it was magic or the end of days coming to make sinners finally pay up. Half of the world seemed to turn to faith near the end. The other half just ran. It probably doesn't help that death is running back at you, screaming and gnashing its teeth.

Scientists were resourceful, and the governments of the world were tenacious. Man might have been able to save most major cities if things hadn't changed. Just before the Internet was struck down, the news story broke on all networks that the dead had changed. *Mutated, evolved, adapted*—all these words were thrown around, but no one actually knew what had caused it. People learned that zombies had become as diverse as any other organism in the world. Reports had come in from South America that there were zombies who could leap like grasshoppers and rain down like locusts onto the living. Europe was reporting some that could rip down walls with acts of monumental strength. North America had many kinds that seemed to show a hive-mind mentality, working together to attack the living. Then China broke news stories that some had supernatural abilities, able to even control and manipulate fire somehow. After footage broke of a zombie pyrokinetically burning a bus full of survivors in Beijing before a horde fed on them, most people knew it was the apocalypse.

After most of the world's networks went down, the infrastructure of North America was ripped apart by the various hordes. Some fought each other while others seemed to just concentrate on the living. Although sun didn't physically affect them, zombies seemed to have a hard time seeing in the light and seemed to despise it. Hordes would hunt at night, and most would disappear into their shaded territories or nests during the day. Because of this, man learned to fear the night and take shelter when sundown came. That was the only way the few remaining learned to survive. They banded together, built high walls and strong buildings, or went underground and always tried to be armed to the teeth. Violence of action wasn't just a term for the military anymore; it was a way of life. This was the world locked between stagnation and crisis mode.

3.

Outskirts of Shytown Trade Line

Zombie Civil Rights Group

Present Day

SUNLIGHT GLANCED OFF the cells of the solar charger on Mason's backpack as the truck he rode in hit a bump, bouncing the bed. "I still don't understand why we couldn't just take the truck we had."

Ashley was watching the road ahead over the back of the cab. She didn't even turn around to respond with, "Because we smashed up the whole front end and it wouldn't drive more than fifty feet. I tried moving it out of the compound, and something was wrong with the wheels."

Mason sighed. He reached up and pulled his hockey mask down off his face. He hadn't had it down since they left the enclave, having used it to keep the sun off his eyes once daylight broke. Staring down at it, he thought the picture he had painted just the night before looked dirty, worn and ancient. He let his thumb scratch a groove across the red paint just to see the line he produced.

"How you holding up?" asked a familiar voice to his left. Mason glanced up and saw Donathan and his wry smile looking back at him from across the truck bed. His duster seemed browner than usual since the road they were on seemed to kick up dust constantly. It seemed to hang in the air and stick to everything like moon dust from those old moon landing films.

Mason shrugged then replied, "Fine... I guess... all things considered. I mean, we're lucky we found a ride away from there so soon, but you don't really trust these guys, do you?"

Donathan seemed to smile a bit more and said, "No, of course not, but we'll be fine. We always are."

That much was true, anyway. Mason had met up with them about three and a half years before, hungry, overheated, and exhausted. They had nursed him back to health and said they'd been scouting for him awhile. Donathan told Mason that all of their parents had been friends long before the zombie invasion had happened and that he had been sent by his dad to reunite them all. When Mason asked if their parents were still alive, he only got long stares from both Ashley and Donathan. He hadn't asked more than once because he really didn't care for the answer. Life had been too long and too shitty to dwell on the past. Besides, he hadn't really known his parents well.

Ashley had talked about her mom some. She had witnessed her being killed one night by a type of zombie Ashley referred to only as "a complete nightmare." She had a single long scar across her left cheek that she said was a reminder from that night to never quit. She never did, no matter how overwhelmed they were. It had saved them on quite a few occasions. On her back, she carried a bat, which was her weapon of choice when things went wrong. She was probably the best shot out of all of them. Even Donathan had commented that her skill with a firearm was "unique," but she didn't prefer to use it.

Donathan was the fastest draw of them all, though. He was the fastest at everything—running, shooting, eating. When he wasn't planning, he was the quickest thing on two feet. It bordered on the supernatural. Hell, it might have been supernatural for all Mason knew. Donathan preferred to use pistols when he could. However, if they were assaulting a nest or bandits, he'd commence the fight with a rifle and switch to pistols as they got closer to the target. He came up with the battle strategies, decided their next course of action, and generally acted as the final decision in all matters. After all, it was he who had found the two of them and actually knew the rest of their parents. He never spoke about what had happened to him, and even though he was smiling most of the time, no one had been brave enough to ask. It was a weight everyone knew he carried.

Looking back down at his feet, Mason noticed all the solar chargers were in the light except his. He lifted his backpack from near his feet and shoved it forward a foot until the sun beamed down on it. They all had actual mp3-player chargers mounted on their backpacks. Two of the chargers were shaped like flowers with three petals, and each of the petals had green-and-black solar panels for drinking in as much charge as they could during the daytime. His, however, was just a square piece of paneling they'd rigged because they couldn't find an official charger for him. That suited him fine, though, as he had painted the shape of the flower petals across the panel to match everyone else's look.

All of their battle strategy was set to music. Donathan had explained to him originally that it was because ancient warriors used to use war drums when going into battle. Not only did this dominate the enemy by showing them that they moved in unison, but the song's highs and lows could also be capitalized on to signal when and where they performed certain actions. Plus, the music helped calm their nerves and make it less like combat and more like a game. It must have worked because none of them seemed to be suffering too terribly after combat. Sure, they had nightmares, but who lived in this world and didn't?

Reaching forward, he unzipped his backpack and began fishing out his various paint bottles. He didn't have any actual paint canisters, so whenever he found a suitable shade of paint, he'd add it to his collection of paint stored in various plastic bottles he'd come across on their adventures. Some of the shades didn't look quite perfect because not every blue was a royal blue and not every yellow was canary yellow, but the mixed enamel did the job, and at least he'd always have paint on hand when he needed it. He always needed it.

Once he'd gathered purple, black, red, and yellow, he reached into one of the front pockets on his bag then slowly and careful pulled out the Four Winter Paintbrush. For a moment, he held it up in the sunlight, admiring the shape of the brown leather handle and puffy, feathered tip. It had been one of his favorite possessions ever since he found it one night when kicking scraps around in a toy store in King City, California. Why there was such an art treasure in a toy store was beyond him, but he wasn't one to question luck; He just embraced it.

Not caring that this was not their truck, he squirted dollops of paint on the wheel hub he was sitting on, then dipped his brush and began working on his mask. He'd never actually know what he was making until it was done; he just sort of shut his mind off and got out of his own way. The paint he was brushing over was thick today, and he'd definitely need to take time out soon to scrape off a few layers, but for the time being, he just continued giving the mask a yellow wash. When it was done, he paused to admire his beaming-yellow creation. He held it up in the dusty desert wind in hopes that it would dry more quickly.

Noticing his happiness, Ashley perked up and rattled it a bit. This was her thing. "What are you going to paint this time? Video game references no one understands anymore? Maybe write a movie one-liner on it? What about puppies?"

That actually made him wince for a moment. This was the longest argument they had ever had. It had been going for years.

"Say what you want about the Puppy Suit, but it is a sound plan," he replied.

Rolling her eyes, she turned her head forward and leaned farther over the cab of the truck as she said in a cold voice, "No. It's not. You're not safe from zombies just because you're wearing a suit made of live puppies. How would that even work, anyway?"

Drawing a breath and preparing for the worst, Mason said, "Look, it's simple: you attach them somehow to your coat with a series of pockets. Just strap them in, and you're good to go. No zombie will attack puppies."

Having been through this before, Ashley added, "Oh, that's right! Remind me again why zombies won't attack puppies?"

"They just won't. I know zombies can register some things, and puppies are clearly cute to everyone. I know zombies aren't as dumb as people think they are because one time I actually made one laugh..." Mason trailed off after his last words because Ashley had turned around and begun mouthing the sentence while he was reciting it. He had told them that several times before, but he knew deep down that no one believed him. Zombies were evil sadistic creatures who couldn't be reasoned with most of the time. Even he agreed with that.

Deciding that his mask was dry, he set it face up across his knee and continued painting it. Lines became curves, and the paint was lighter on some edges but darker on the ones that curved under. He would eventually decide something was good and move on to the next part. It was a ritual, and he had decided long ago that nothing had to be perfect but everything had to be good.

Ashley perked up and said, "So what's our next move in finding the Princess?"

Donathan, still smiling and admiring Mason's work, replied, "Last rumor we had heard was that she was near a beach in Half Moon Bay. I don't know if it'll take a week or a month to get there at the rate we're going, but we're definitely going to need to make our next stop a town. We need supplies."

Mason groaned as the word *town* was said but didn't pause to look up from his work.

Smiling and looking back, Ashley remarked, "Ohh-hh, that's right. You don't like towns because bad things always happen in them."

Mason just continued painting and glanced up slightly in Ashley's direction.

Ashley's eyes dropped a little, and she added, "Did you catch I said *Princess*? That was your cue to add, 'Your princess is in another castle' like that old Mario game."

Mason refocused on his work and continued painting. Ashley was fairly annoyed at this point and said, "Are you listening to me?"

Without looking up, Mason replied, "I... art."

Suddenly, the truck came to a screeching halt, and all the occupants in the bed looked up curiously. Ashley's eyes darted around, trying to figure out what was going on. "Why are we stopped next to this huge cliff?" she asked.

"Strange things are afoot at the Circle K," Mason added in an unamused tone as he looked back down and continued painting.

Donathan said, "And back to his normal self. I imagine we're abou—" but was cut off suddenly when the two men who had been driving the truck stepped out of the cab in unison, strolled past, and lowered the tailgate of the truck while holding something shiny.

"Don't move a damned muscle," the fat man said with angst in his voice. "Eddie, get those weapons."

The skinny man was wearing a flannel shirt with the sleeves ripped off and a white t-shirt under it. Mason finally looked up from his finished painting as they dragged his machine gun out from under his legs. "What's going on?" he asked in a dumbfounded voice.

Ashley said, "Welcome to the party, buttercup; just the usual robbery and shakedown. Other than that, I can't complain."

"Shaddup and get off the truck," the fat man said. Eddie backed up to let Mason and Donathan jump down. Ashley hesitated a moment at the edge and then held up a hand, motioning to Eddie that she needed help down.

Without hesitating, Eddie took her hand and politely helped her down.

The fat man became angry and waved the rifle in her face while shouting, "Damn it, Eddie, knock it off! We're supposed to be robbing them!"

Eddie replied in a whiny voice, "But it's just not polite, Francis," then was cut off by the fat man correcting him.

"FRANKIE. It's Frankie, EDDIE. No one calls me Francis. Now get their cash out of those damned bags." His chubby fingers gripped the underside of the rifle's barrel as he turned and motioned for the rest of them to push back toward the cliff. He was wearing a very inappropriate outfit of khaki shorts, sandals, and a blue t-shirt. His tangled blond hair and chubby face made him look less like a bandit and more like a washed-up surfer from the west coast.

After a few minutes of standing there while Eddie sifted through their belongings, his voice from the back of the truck said, "Frankie, they have music player things here."

Frankie adopted a frustrated tone. "Why do we care? I'm not going to take their last belongings. I'm a criminal but not a complete jackass." As he said this, he grinned slightly, raised the rifle's aim toward the sky and took a bow.

Donathan kept his same steely gaze and smile as Ashley replied, "Oh, so you'll just take our weapons, ammunition, and cash and leave us for dead in the middle of a desert, midday; charmed, I'm sure."

Frankie's gaze turned sinister as he re-aimed the rifle at her head and said, "At least it's not nightfall, right missy?"

Mason sighed and hung the mask back on his head, keeping its picture skyward so it could keep the sun off his eyes as they continued waiting for Eddie to finish searching their items.

Finally, he kicked all of their belongings off the back, climbed down off the truck, tucked a handful of cash into his pocket, and picked up all of their weapons in an awkward way so his arms were completely full.

Taking the cue, Frankie barked orders at the rest of them. "We're taking the cash and the weapons. Turn around and walk, keeping the cliff on your right side."

The three of them began walking, Mason half stepping, half kicking dust with his right foot out of annoyance. The sun was hot, and this was completely bothersome. After they had gone about one hundred feet, Donathan leaned across to Ashley and whispered, "I think this has gone on long enough." They all stopped, turned around, and faced their robbers.

At their defiance, Frankie shouted, "Hey! I'll do it. I'll... light you up... you know!"

Donathan just smiled back and nodded as Ashley reached over her head and pulled out the baseball bat.

Seeing this, Frankie said, "So what? It's a bat. I have a gun, for Christ's sake!"

Ashley pulled out two baseballs from a small hidden pouch hanging off her waistline near her left leg.

Mason turned toward her. "I bet you can't on the first try."

Her eyes lowered for a moment, an evil grin spreading across her face.

Frankie was still yelling at them at the top of his lungs while Eddie just stood there staring, with a dopey look on his face.

Squinting his eyes, Frankie continued his loud rant, "I swear... I'll gut every last one of you. Leave you here as zombie bait and pawn the last of your belongings as—"

A loud crack was heard, and Frankie looked up just in time to see a ball whiz past his face and thud into the sand next to him. It rolled two more feet and finally came to rest, showing two words written on it, Fuck You.

"Hey, that almost hit me! I swear to God, I will—"

The crack was much louder the second time, and another ball connected with Frank's head then bounced to Eddie's feet, revealing the word Seriously. Frank swayed a moment, then fell over, stirring up a large cloud of dust. Laughter could be heard as Mason yelled, "Bonk!"

Angry, Eddie shouted while still looking down, "Hey! Not okay! Did you forget we have all your guns?" His last word seemed to lag out as he looked up, trying to figure out the curious whistling noise coming toward him. For a split second, his eyes focused on a baseball bat falling out of the sky and smashing into his face. Guns scattered everywhere as he fell back into the truck. Then he trotted forward two forceful steps before collapsing face first onto the sand.

"Fhkkk seek. Luke aht me. Shiek it off already."

The ringing in Eddie's ears subsided as he opened his eyes and audibly gasped. His head felt as though he'd been hit by a bus.

In a hushed tone, Frankie asked, "Eddie, are you awake? Christ, wake up. I can't see, Eddie. What can you see?"

"Ya... ya, I'm here Frankie. I... can't seem to move," Eddie said in a confused voice.

"That's because we're tied together, idiot. I'm behind you, facing that cliff we parked next to. I can't stand up with you tied to me, neither. Listen, we're only about a foot away, so let's just try and edge away slowly so as they don't notice us doing it," replied Frankie.

"Yeah, that's a good idea. They're over by the truck right now discussing something. Say when."

Frank drew a breath, preparing to move. "Now!" he said, and they both tried to jump but only shifted about an inch to the side.

Sounding concerned, Eddie said, "Frankie, I think I jumped late. Let's try that again."

"Now!" Frankie announced. They both tried to hop and scoot but only moved an inch in the other direction, back to where they started.

"This isn't working, Frankie. Let's try standing up."

They both pulled their knees into their chests then flexed their legs and pushed, using the other person as a counterweight. After some huffing and wheezing, they managed to stand up and both cheered at the same time. Then as Frankie stepped sideways to rotate them around, he came face to face with Ashley, who was staring at him ominously from only a foot away.

"Need a hand?" she asked as she kicked Frankie's legs out from under him and sent both men sprawling back onto the ground.

Footsteps came closer as Donathan's voice came from one side, "Get them up, Ash. I need to have a word."

The small Asian girl reached down, took a firm grip on the knot, and yanked both men up with force.

Frankie nervously stared Donathan's half smile in the face. Eddie's head kept bobbing left and right, trying to look over his shoulders to get a view of Donathan.

"Hi, my name's Donathan," he said, and motioning behind himself, he added, "My friend by your truck is

Mason, and you've already met Ashley."

"Uhh... charmed?" Frankie added in a confused tone, mimicking Ashley's comment from earlier in the day.

Without hesitating, Eddie said, "It's a pleasure to meet you."

"Knock it off. I'm Frankie, and this is Eddie. Listen we didn—"

Holding a hand up that silenced Frankie, Donathan said, "Frank... you tried to rob us, but you didn't take everything. I'm going to assume you might have a family?"

Frank nodded forcefully, "Yes... a huge... huge family."

Eddie added, "The biggest. He's got two kids," right as Frank remarked that he had three kids.

Eddie backpedaled and said he meant three kids as Frank said that Eddie thought of his dog as a kid.

Finally, both men just stopped talking. Donathan's smile actually widened a bit before he said, "You didn't try to murder us or steal everything we had, so we're not going to kill you—"

Frankie interrupted, "Oh, thank you so much—"

Donathan finished with, "We're just going to take your truck."

"Son of a BITCH!" Frankie shouted.

It was a hot day, and the nearest town was at least ten miles away.

"We've tied the rope to the back of the truck, and as we drive off, that knot should unfurl so that you can find your way out of the desert." Turning to walk back toward the truck, Donathan said, "I'm going to leave a canteen here in the sand so when you come untied, you at least have some water for the trip back."

Just then, Ashley got an evil look on her face, extended her right leg as hard as she could into Frank's side, and kicked both men off the cliff.

Donathan dropped the canteen, then turned around to look at the men only to find Ashley standing there with a shocked look on her face. She shrugged her shoulders and leaned forward as she quietly mumbled, "They tripped."

"Uhh... The knot definitely came undone," came a shout from over the edge of the cliff. Dust scattered as Ashley, Mason, and Donathan all ran to peer over.

"Damn it," Ashley said when she saw both men hanging on to the unfurled rope.

In a fear-filled voice, Frankie said, "Please pull us up. Please, I'll... please help," and Eddie echoed him every time he said the word 'please.'

With a look of excitement and realization, Ashley sprinted off and jumped into the cab of the truck, starting it up before Mason and Donathan had even finished turning around.

Mason just pulled his mask down to reveal the image of a cartoon squirrel screaming, his hands pressed up against the temples of his furry head.

Donathan shouted, "Ash, wait—"

The tires sputtered sand and dust everywhere as Ashley jammed on the gas pedal and shouted, "Too late; can't hear!" followed by something about "ear dyslexia." The truck hesitated for a second before dashing across the desert and away from the cliff. The two men hanging by the rope could be heard screaming as they sped upward toward the edge of the cliff.

"Who waits to rob people until their getaway vehicle has only half a gallon of gas?" Ashley asked as they trotted away from the quiet truck, leaving it to rust out in the desert.

Mason just shrugged, put his mask up and said, "No idea. Do you think they'll have any art supplies in the next town?"

"Did you miss the part where I just saved our lives back there?" she snapped at him.

Interrupting the argument about to ensue, Donathan said, "I think Myriad or Barstow is not too far to the south."

Mason asked, "Which one is the name it was called before the plague?"

Donathan remarked, "No idea. I haven't been out this way in years." He then took a deep breath and said in an amused way, "Towns wind up getting renamed out here so much, you could become a resident of a new town without ever moving away."

After walking through the sand for another ten minutes, Ashley asked, "Do you think we'll find word about Princess Jae when we get to Myriad?"

Donathan answered, "Probably not. Last we heard, she was in Half Moon Bay. That's weeks to the north."

Princess Jae was the nickname for Jessica Pulse, the last known friend of all their parents. Donathan had been searching for all of them for years, but every time they got to a location where Princess Jae was rumored to be, she was gone, and the trail had gone cold. Of everyone they had ever hunted down, chasing her was most like chasing a ghost.

"We have to find her eventually," whispered Mason. They had been going up and down the Shytown Conglomerate Trail for almost three years and never once laid eyes on her. They had heard occasional whispers of how elusive she was, too.

Ashley kicked a rock down the road and jogged two feet forward before adding, "In her defense, she has no idea who we are. She probably just thinks we're bounty hunters or assassins."

That was probably true. They hadn't exactly been quiet on their jaunt down the trade line. Aside from revisiting some sites from their past, they had a nasty habit of getting in trouble and attracting attention everywhere they went. Mason was so obsessed with art that he once blew up half an enclave and tore down most of their defenses just so he could see the pictures inside. Before the undead had arrived, it had been a museum. Thankfully, no one was killed that night, but he couldn't be reasoned with when it came to art or visual stimuli. The group had learned to work around this quirk.

Ashley wasn't much better. If someone wronged them, her rage would carry them to hell and back. Thankfully, she was always so focused that when she really lost her cool, she became a juggernaut of force and determination.

That, combined with the fact that they kept revisiting towns and enclaves from their past, certainly didn't help things.

"Do you think this town will have pancakes?" Mason asked in a curious voice.

"Do they ever?" Ashley replied.

4.

Rift Parish

Mason

Five Years Earlier

"PERHAPS THEY'LL HAVE PANCAKES," Ethan said with enthusiasm, walking toward the enclave. They were three days north of Bakersfield on the Shytown Trail and trying to find shelter as the sun crept down low in the sky.

Mason turned to look at his companions. Ethan towered over most. A kind man, rare to find in the world as it was these days, he stood at six feet one and had a wide belly and a long face half hidden by a scraggly beard. It was black and matched what little hair he had left on the top of his head. Once, one of the other orphans had asked him about his baldness, and he had replied, "I'm not bald, child. I've just grown through my hair." He always seemed lighthearted, and Mason often wondered if he did it for the other kids. Ethan wore a square-shouldered brown leather jacket, obviously quite old, and long green slacks. He also had a white scarf around his neck even when it was hot. It never seemed to hang quite right, always looking bunched up and giving him this Renaissance feel to his fashion. Strung across his back was a small gray satchel backpack that had short, thin straps and a somewhat feminine quality to it. The image was always reinforced whenever he had a fit of laughter, which could only be described as jolly.

Mason was one of six orphans who were moving to a small town, formerly known as Merced, California. He didn't know most of their names. In fact, he was really only close to one.

Heather was almost as old as him and about five feet three inches tall. Her blond hair managed to stay mostly straight and untangled even in the face of the end of days. Their age meant that they'd probably never be adopted since they were both almost 15. She had always told him that was fine with her. She'd just start working for the corporation that ran the orphanage and work her way up to a real life. He had always told her that sounded like a great idea, not because he wanted to work for a corporation, but because it meant keeping his only friend in the world since he had met her last year.

Her looks sort of reminded him of what little he could remember about his mother. She was tiny, lean, and blond. Her tiny ears and full lips gave her elfin features. Her smile was warm and inviting, and he would always remember her talking with an accent and gesturing with her hands for emphasis.

He only knew his parents up until he was six years old. Before that, his life was all Saturday morning cartoons, movies, and playing video games with his dad. His dad had been addicted to video games, mostly vintage ones. Everything he liked had to do with pop culture. He had always referred to movies and video games as "the evolution of story." It seemed like a silly thing to remember, but Mason could never get that term out of his head.

He longed for those days before the plague. Everything was so happy and simple then. As they neared the enclave and saw men working around the razor wire, walls, and open gate out front, Mason fought to force those final images of his family out of his head. He didn't want to remember them. He only had bits and pieces of them anyway, so why should they matter? After a few more steps, he just gave in and let the pain wash over him.

It had been the end of summer when they stopped airing Saturday morning cartoons and he'd finally taken notice of the rest of the world. The news broadcasts seemed to announce the worst, and he remembered asking his parents if they were okay. His father had just smiled and told him that of course they were.

Dad had always seemed to have a lot of confidence, but when Mason looked back, he began to think it was all for show to keep his family calm. At least his dad knew the number one rule in life, panic is contagious. The world panicked, of course. If the zombies weren't destroying the cities, riots and looting were. The day their building caught fire was the same day he'd lost contact with his folks. All he could really remember about them was the look on his mother's face as she was dragged off into a crowd of people that had surrounded them on the streets. His dad, of course tried to push them through the crowd to find her, but it was far too late, and there were too many people then.

The one time he had seen real terror on his dad's face was when the crowd began running all around them. Shoving and pressure instantly became trampling and screams as people fought for their lives to get through the twisting mass of humans. Fear-filled shouts of "Zombies!" rose up from the crowd as people came under attack from a horde emerging from alleyways and nearby streets. When the crowd did finally part, it left Mason and his dad standing face-to-face with one of the undead as it swayed back and forth in a ripped white sweater covered with blood from the arterial spray from his last victim. His one eye darted all around as the other was just a hollow eye socket. A second later that spastic eye came to rest on the pair of them. Dad seemed to know what was about to happen, so he shoved Mason behind him as the crowd dashed in various directions like rats fleeing to their holes. The last thing Dad ever said was, "Run." He then balled his fists, slid one leg back, rotated his hips forward in a quick motion as the zombie lunged, and with a sound like someone hitting frozen meat, smashed the zombie in the face.

Mason could still see that one zombie falling backward, his head thrown back as teeth and pieces of necrotic flesh rained down around him. In Mason's head, he could still envision Dad slowly rotating his hips in the other direction to swing his left hand into another zombie as the sky and street darkened from the horde lunging at him from all directions. Even insects didn't swarm like the undead did toward living flesh. That was the last thing Mason remembered of his family.

With luck and a few close calls, he'd wound up in an orphanage in a town with walls like a fortress, but he couldn't remember much about the months in between, and that suited him just fine.

"Excuse me, good sir. I'm tasked with moving these orphans to a new compound, and we're seeking shelter for the night. Is there a chance we could rest here tonight? We have coin." Why did everything Ethan said seem as if it was coming from medieval times?

A man with long stringy hair and a glass eye opened his mouth in shock and just continued to make the same face in Ethan's direction. He looked completely confused by everything just said.

A person wearing a smudged gray shirt stepped out from inside the enclave's dark interior and said, "Absolutely! You'll have to excuse Jed's attitude. We're not entirely sure if he's just slow or suffered a stroke a few years back." Then pausing to draw a breath, he added, "Jed, please continue on with your work."

Jed, his eyes still focused on Ethan, slowly closed his mouth and tugged at the wire in one of his gloved hands to continue stringing it across the enclave's front defenses.

Stepping forward past the other workers, who seemed equally annoyed with the newcomers, Ethan extended his hand. "Pleased to meet you; Ethan Josephus. It's always a pleasure to meet a gentleman while one is traveling."

Taking his hand and shaking it for a second with force while his eyes squinted a bit and his smile widened, the man in the gray shirt replied, "Dan. But people around here call me Big Dan."

"Who calls you Big Dan?" another voice asked, and a shorter man with white hair limped out of the enclave.

Anger spread across Dan's face for a split second before he calmly added, "Father..." He glanced back at the kids. "These travelers are looking for a place to bed down for the night."

"Name's Aaron," the man with the white hair said to Ethan while nodding slightly. "No one calls me 'Big.' We don't have any room for travelers, but I've heard there's a villa an hour north of here that might."

Ethan's smile faded away for a second. "I don't think there's an hour of sunlight left."

"I'm sure we could clear them some floor on the north side, away from the pens," Dan said while turning to face Aaron.

Aaron glared back for a moment before saying, "Naw, can't do it."

Ethan began to add something while taking a step forward when Dan interrupted, speaking in a hushed tone, "We need to... Dad. You know... help." The last word was said with force and a bit of angst as if to reinforce his point. Still keeping his eyes on Aaron, Dan slightly nodded his head in Ethan's direction.

Aaron inhaled, then held the breath in for a second before nodding weakly and turning to limp back into the compound.

Waiting a moment and letting his eyes follow his father's path back inside, Dan finally turned to the orphans before holding up a hand to direct them through the dark doors inside. "Kids, what do you know about harvesting zombies?"

5.

Falling Sands

The Judge

Present Day

THE COLOR AND SHADE of the ceiling and floor matched the wood-paneled walls perfectly, giving everything a regal feeling. Although the box of a room had no windows, large oil paintings with ornate gold frames covered the center of the back wall and both sides. The door in the only wall without a frame had a golden doorway that seemed to match the same pattern that adorned the frames.

Off to one side was a large dark mahogany bookshelf with various volumes of the forgotten world strewn across it, along with various steel, silver, and gold knick-knacks. In the center of the room was a massive desk with more random, revered "office junk" on it. The desk had been pushed forward to make room for the sliding recliner that housed the chest-heaving, sweaty, overweight owner of the room.

The man's large cheeks shook steadily as he snored. His small glasses heaved back and forth as if his nose was somehow a tremulous ocean during a great storm. A small creak issued from the door as it opened, announcing someone's presence, which caused the man to wake with a frustrated shriek. "Yes? What?"

A younger man with a receding hairline poked his head in just long enough to announce, "Judge, Lady Mary Helen of the Protectorate Security Forces here to see you—" His last word was almost cut off as he was shoved aside by two soldiers clad in form-fitting body armor that made their biceps shiny and their pecs gigantic. Their masks had dark, ominous eyes triangular in shape, angled down towards each other, giving the illusion of a sharp and sinister stare. On each mask, a breathing apparatus with an open mouth and holes showed a small grill behind. One tube snaked down from the side over each man's left shoulder and into what the Judge knew to be a small pack behind the back, used to filter oxygen in the dirty and less tamed areas of the world, as well as to cool the head of the user wearing the exoskeleton. Each mask was black, with the exception of the small frame around functional parts of the mask, which was obviously made of copper that had begun to show through the paint after so many years of service.

One man stepped through into the room and off to the side as another held the door open for a petite woman to step through. She wore a similar suit, except hers was white—and the trimming around the edges of her armor had strips painted blue—and had slight curves to it, as was normal for a female's uniform. Obviously, she'd taken the time and care to repaint over it, as her uniform looked less worn and disheveled. Although small in stature, she took confident, long strides, loping into the room and carrying a small tan file folder in her right hand. She didn't wear a helmet like the other soldiers. Dark hair, cropped short to her chin, was parted in the middle and would leave her an attractive, almost cherubic, youthful appearance if it weren't for the fact she had a dark, tortured frown on her face, and her eyes looked as if war was screaming through them. She snapped to attention but kept that rage in her eyes as the second man stepped through the doorway and stood on her other side with a quickness that could only be described as a military standard.

The Judge had known her for several years, and even though she was tightly wound, she was also extremely efficient at producing results. In fact, he relied on her for most of the footwork these days. Other groups he had at his disposal were less dedicated and often tended to follow their own guidelines. Of course, he usually sent for her, and she rarely would consider disturbing him unless it was a pressing matter, so he just sighed and shuffled random items from one side of his desk to another for a moment before clearing his throat to let her know he was ready to continue.

As Mary Helen spoke, the Judge sensed that even her methodical tone sounded as if it was marching with a sense of purpose.

"We have a witness from the massacre at Rift Parrish," she said.

Leaning back a moment to feign deep thought, the Judge asked, taking the time to parse out each word slowly in an elegant manner, "Remind me again; what happened at Rift Parish?"

The woman didn't look surprised as she stated very bluntly, "Small harvester operation further north of our trade line that was hit by raiders. Originally thought to be a massacre due to all of the bodies found. We now know that most of the people were there during the initial attack. We have one of the survivors just outside—"

"Yes, yes, fine. Send him in," the Judge blurted out.

The woman stepped aside, and framed in the doorway was a tan, balding man wearing a faded prison jumper and jeans. The man nervously nodded his head to the interior of the room as the Judge beckoned him in.

A warm voice issued from the Judge's pristine mouth, which had instantly donned a wide friendly smile. "Come in! Come in! Boy! What a pleasure it is to meet one of our fine employees! I can't tell you how sorry I am for what you went through. Have you ever had our conglomerate's brand of cigars? They come from tobacco fields grown east of here, and I do not kid you in saying the weather in that valley is well tempered indeed; they are simply heaven!" He quickly opened and shut a drawer of the desk, producing a fat, greasy, dark-brown cigar, which he offered forward, rolling his wrist in a ritualistic fashion toward the tan man.

As the man mumbled a thank-you and reached up to take the cigar, the Judge leaned forward sourly and scolded him with "Ah ah ah ah," followed by a quick demand, "Your name, sir!"

Lowering his head and snatching back his hand to place it defensively in the other, the man stammered, "J-Jackson, your majesty, sir," before looking up slowly to meet the Judge's gaze.

Still looking stern, the Judge nodded in the direction of the cigar until Jackson slowly reached up and took it from the Judge's left hand.

"'The Judge' is the only name and title you need to know—or 'Your Honor' if you prefer. I am named for what I do and for the fact that I send good men to their fortunes and our enemies to their death. I will thank you to remember that as you address me." After Jackson nodded and lowered his eyes toward the base of the desk, the Judge finally relaxed back in his chair and let his face drift back into a perverse sneer. "So Jackson, what happened at your enclave?" His voice had become friendly again.

Still refusing to make eye contact, Jackson told what had transpired. He went into detail about how the invaders had breached the walls using a driverless vehicle, which had taken quite a bit of fire from the guard towers. Continuing on, he touched on how the three people who rushed through the newly made opening had seemed almost possessed by ability in the firefight as music from the vehicle blasted into the night. Finally, he explained how they had shot the enclave's leader and all the zombies they had caged before moving the other employees to the roof and informing them that when daylight came, they would no longer work there and were to return home and take up new employment as something less destructive.

The Judge did his best to hide the shock and confusion that had crept across his face by the end of the man's story. "So, they just killed some employees to get to the entire stock of undead and then told the rest of you, you no longer worked for us?"

Jackson nodded meekly. "Yes, sir."

"Strange." The Judge paused for a moment to gather his wits and make sure his voice readopted its faux-rich melody. "Well, I am... sorry you went through that, Jackson. You'll no doubt want a transfer approved for White-cap's harvester enclave immediately…" His voice trailed off as he realized the man hadn't agreed with him in either voice or body language.

"N-no, no, Judge. I—"

"I'm sorry?" the Judge asked with force.

"I would like t-to… go work for a farmer enclave. You know, learn a new skill." Jackson mumbled quietly.

In the back of the room, Mary Helen cleared her voice and sniffed quietly, signaling to the Judge that she disliked discontent.

The Judge cocked his head toward Jackson as if showing that he agreed with Mary Helen's nonverbal message. "So you? Want? A new? Type of employment?"

Jackson just nodded.

Leaning back farther in his chair, the Judge smiled. "Jackson, do you have a family?"

"I'm sorry?" Jackson said.

"A family… a child, a wife, perhaps a dog." After Jackson shook his head no, the Judge gave a sigh that almost seemed relieved. "So you want us to retrain you and give you a new job after we've lost an entire enclave's profit. Hell, we'd even have to relocate you, Jackson—"

Sensing distress, Jackson interrupted, "No sir, I… can pay for me moving to the new enclave."

Smiling widely, the Judge replied with a warm tone, "Ohhh, you can pay relocation fees? Why didn't you just say so? I will sign the papers and have you moved to one of our farming enclaves immediately. Please report to Hines in our north compound near the front gate. He will handle everything."

Suddenly grinning, Jackson nodded his head, thanking the Judge, and backed out of the room past Mary Helen. She just slid aside to allow him through and glared at his departure before snapping back to attention in the center of the room.

After waiting for Jackson's footfalls to fade sufficiently down the hallway, the Judge produced a microphone and announced in a voice that echoed through speakers all over the compound, "Co-ad-ju-tant... co-adjutant," being sure to pronounce the syllables in a monotonous manner. The younger fellow with the receding hairline stuck his head back in the doorway. His sudden appearance made the Judge jump in surprise before he steadied himself and said, "Boy, run ahead of that fellow who just left, and inform Hines that he has a new recruit for the slave pens." The young man darted out of sight instantly. As the sound of the man drifted off down the hallway, he added nonchalantly to the rest of the room, "Retraining is expensive, but a slave can mine a pretty penny almost immediately."

Then sighing and shifting around in his chair, the Judge said, "Lady Mary, what can you tell me about this group of fools who dare to steal from our profits?"

Sticking her chest out and tilting her head back, Mary replied in her reporting voice, "Just that they're called the Zombie Civil Rights group or ZCR for short."

The Judge was shocked. "The Zombie Civil Rights group?"

Making eye contact, she continued, "Yes, Judge." She paused to draw a breath, then said, "We've asked some other enclaves about it and managed to find one individual who knows them. She claimed the name is just a joke between its three members. They aren't actual zombie activists."

"Well that's... good?" he asked, and she nodded in response. "But how did you know what their name is?"

"They wrote it down, Judge. On the walls."

"On the walls? So they wanted you to know this was an attack?" The man looked frustrated at this point as if he didn't want to be bothered with understanding this situation.

"We're not sure, Your Honor. They also repainted an old stop sign out front of the enclave backwards so it said POTS and then stuck kitchen pots around the base of it. And they decorated the decimated zombie pens with Christmas decorations."

"But it's July, isn't it?" The Judge boggled.

Speaking slowly, as if not understanding if this was a serious question, she answered, "Yes, Judge. It's July." She nodded, then said, "We've been able to follow them up the Shytown Trail. It seems they leave a trail of art everywhere they go."

"Art? As in," he gestured to the rest of the room and continued, "my beautiful oil paintings of the gorgeous world we live in?"

Her frown seemed to deepen as her eyes took in the pictures of similar green hills with the plain sun shining down on them in each separate painting.

"Yes, sort of," she replied.

Pausing for a moment, the Judge looked up as if deep in thought. Mary Helen drew in a breath and straightened her shoulders for the third time, having been through this before.

"Well, then." The Judge lowered his gaze to meet hers and placed one of his chubby hands firmly on the desk in front of him as he leaned forward. "I suppose something will have to be done about these artists."

6.

Bantam Town

Zombie Civil Rights Group

Present Day

"GAME FACES ON," Donathan reminded them. They strode forward with him in the lead, Ashley behind him and to the left and Mason on the other side of her.

Mason quietly asked, "What does that mean again?"

"It means look badass so no one screws with us." She glanced over at him while giving him a smart-assed smile and said, "Basically, don't be yourself."

"I hope you get sand in your vagina," he replied.

She stopped midstep and gave him a stunned look.

"Ya, I said it." He smiled widely as he continued walking forward past her stunned face.

"Children, please," Donathan said in a dry tone. "We're trying to look menacing here."

Dust settled, stirred up, and hung around their ankles as they walked. Ashley's dress flicked forward in the slight breeze stirred up by their movements. As the town spread out before them, dust-filled streets gave way to rusted sheet metal mixed with wooden walls and roofs. Faded red and pockmarked white seemed to be the dominant colors on most of the wooden buildings. Brown planks with edges rounded from years of wear formed sidewalks that surrounded each building and lined the street.

When Ashley looked in Mason's direction again, he had slung his machine gun farther behind him and was walking along holding a paintbrush in his mouth while trying to pull paint out of his backpack with one hand and holding his mask with the other. She raised an eyebrow as he fumbled around with his items for a moment, and then she slapped his mask out of his hand. Donathan stopped walking, dropped his smile, and blinked for a moment, staring forward before finally turning his head slowly to see what chaos was going on. Mason had already put his items away and, with a guilty look on his face, was standing back up after stooping down to pick up his mask.

Ashley noticed it first; this town had a beat. Children ran alongside them, excitedly rambling and asking questions. Chickens across the street were squawking in a melodic manner. People's shoes and boots walking on either side of them down the sidewalks seemed to have an excited repetition to their step. Wind chimes rang out in an echoing pitch that had life to it.

Reaching down, she produced two earbuds that had been wedged into the hemline of her dress. Reaching behind her left side, she cued up a song labeled "Doomtree – Low Light Low Life" and tapped "play" on her mp3 player, letting the bass sound and rhythmic voice of hip-hop carry her steps forward. Donathan heard the music cue up quietly behind him and knew what had happened without even looking back. As much as he tried to force it away, his smile returned.

"Can I help you?" a man wearing a tan t-shirt and brown trousers asked from the sidewalk. As Donathan turned to face him, he noticed the man's skin was dark red from his hairline down to his wrists. Usually, only farmers who spent most of their time out in the field had this sort of sunburn. Good. Honest people, Donathan thought.

"This town on Shytown's trading trail?" Donathan asked with almost a country ring to his voice.

The man wrinkled his nose and closed one eye for a moment and turned his head down. After spitting, he looked up and said, "Aye. I guess it is. Why? You from the Conglomerate?"

Shaking his head slightly, Donathan said, "No sir. Just hunters looking for work."

The man cocked his head to one side and raised an eyebrow. "Hunters, huh?" After pausing for another moment, the man added, "Well, we're not a big town, so we ain't got a lot of money to offer you, but if it's work you're looking for, we've a nest of Ravens up to the north in the foothills. They've given us trouble for years, and that land they're occupying is damn fertile."

Without hesitating, Donathan said, "That'd be fine."

"WHAT?" Ashley was screaming over the sound of her music before reaching up to remove her earbuds. "Did he just say Ravens?" she asked with a shocked tone.

Mason's eyes widened as he swung his head in Ashley's direction, finally realizing what was going on. "Ravens? Like actual Ravens?"

Walking up with a warm manner, the man extended his hand to Donathan. "Eli's the name, and we sure appreciate hunters in these parts. Well, that is, good hunters. You are good hunters, aren't you?" Eli asked.

"Pleased to meet you Eli, I'm Donathan, and yes... we are skilled. Well, skilled enough to live on, anyway."

While Ashley was still staring frantically at the back of Donathan's head, Mason stepped up on the other side of the men. "I don't like Ravens," he said.

Ignoring him completely, Eli said to Donathan, "It's just we've never actually had hunters come back from there. Not sure if they've been scared off or taken by the Ravens. It'd sure be nice to have someone come back. It only pays $200. Afraid that's all we have."

Donathan nodded, then slapped some dust off his leg. "That'd be fine."

Ashley groaned to Donathan, "D, this is bullshit."

Mason just sighed and quietly said, "I really don't like Ravens."

7.

Rift Parish

Mason

Five Years Earlier

"THE ZOMBIE, CHILDREN, is the bread and butter of our enclave." Dan announced as he walked the wide-eyed children through the compound toward one of the aisles on the far side. "On the other side of our compound, sectioned off, most of our zombie crop are housed."

A young black girl asked, "Why would anyone want to keep zombies?"

Dan smiled at the children and, enjoying the unexpected attention during a workday, said, "Well, science enclaves near us, usually housing a team of scientists, pay top dollar for them to do weird experiments and such."

Several of the kids shouted out, "Gross!"

Dan ignored their exclamations of disgust and continued, "Most people think it's because they're trying to find a way to stop zombies from spreading." He then leaned forward toward the same girl who had asked the question and spoke in a slow whisper, "But me? I think it's because they're monsters themselves, and that they got us into this mess in the first place, and eventually they're going to create... A SUPER ZOMBIE!"

The kids screamed as he shouted the last words. Many of them scattered and ran back to hide behind Ethan. For once, even Ethan looked nervous. The day was almost over, and shadows had begun to creep longer in the already-dark warehouse.

Dusty oversized shelves were everywhere, storing everything from lawn equipment to children's toys, and they stretched up almost out of sight, leading to re-inforced shelving that was obviously mounted to help build up defense for the upper parts of this structure. They could be seen snaking off in all directions overhead, and occasional footsteps rang down from their aluminum planks. Mason knew that even if this place was airtight, they would still keep few lights on at night because they had a tendency to draw in hordes. One or two outside lights were okay. They still would get attacked occasionally, but by nothing an enclave of this size couldn't hold back. However, if the place looked like a party full of life, un-life would soon be knocking at the gates, looking to crawl inside.

"You can sleep back here in this corner," Dan said firmly to Ethan. "There's a bathroom down and to the left in that old garden area with all the dead plants and such." He seemed to take great pleasure in saying the word dead. "And of course, I don't need to stress the safety of the children, so try not to wander off."

Dan finished talking, turned, and walked back down the aisle and off to the left into the "old garden area." The kids were all silent until he walked away, and then a murmur spread throughout the group about how weird this place was. A couple had already begun peering into the different shelves, trying to see what they could find, when Ethan stepped up to curtail that behavior, "Children, leave our hosts' items alone. After all, they were courteous enough to let us stay."

Mason turned to Heather to ask her what she thought of all this, but she answered his question before he opened his mouth. "This place is scary," she said as she glanced up at the shelves and slowly turned around to eyeball the items above.

His breath caught in his throat. He glanced around to see if any of the other kids had noticed what he had noticed yet. Then he took extra care to make sure Ethan was busy calming one of the other children before he reached out his hand to one of the shelves and took hold of the object. He took a deep breath and finally pulled a pencil from the shelf and stuffed it into his pants pocket. If another kid had noticed it, there would no doubt be an argument over it later, and he would either be punished for stealing it or, worse, forced to share it. Neither would be all right in Mason's eyes.

Heather finally stopped studying the upper part of the enclave and looked back at Mason. "What do you think night's like when there are zombies in the same building?"

Mason shivered. He hadn't even thought of it until then. "Do you think we'll be able to hear them?" he asked.

Heather's eyes lit up in a strange way when he asked the question.

"Nonsense," Ethan added, obviously having overheard the conversation, "and even if we can, these fine gentlemen will keep us safe." He gave a reassuring smile and then turned to the rest of the children, "Just remember not to wander off, kids."

Under his breath, Mason asked in a dumbfounded tone, "Who the hell would wander off?"

Heather just smiled back at him.

Mason woke to someone shaking him and jerked up in fright to see Heather smiling back at him. "I want to go see them," she said.

For a moment, Mason had no idea where he was. He sat back, blinking away sleep and pondering where he was and trying to remember the hours before. Shortly after Mason had found the pencil, Ethan had produced some bread from his satchel and, after handing it out to all the children, wandered off to see if he could barter a water jug off the enclave employees. During the twenty minutes he was gone, Mason had laughed and joked with Heather, dug through one of the shelves, gotten into a fistfight with a kid two years younger than him, and managed to hide off to the side of the group, feigning frustration from the fight so he could doodle a pattern on the cement with the pencil. He had somehow managed to keep it hidden from everyone and, in an effort to preserve his slice of heaven, had forced himself to stash it away after just a couple of minutes. It had honestly taken every bit of strength in his being to put the pencil back into his pocket. He still occasionally reached down to check that it was still there.

After night had fallen, the compound had announced they were exercising "light discipline" and had turned most everything off inside, leaving only a few lights to illuminate the dark and musty warehouse.

As Mason sat up, he noticed that except for the occasional moan and shuffling, the whole compound had fallen silent. He couldn't even hear people moving along the catwalk scaffolding above. He stared away from Heather to the end of the aisle that linked the actual warehouse to the garden area. Small moths flickered in semi-circles around a large box with a tow-hook on the front and a light mounted on top of it, shining brightly but making the rest of the dark warehouse look more foreboding. Mason recognized the piece of machinery from old construction sites they had passed along the way, some kind of a square oversized light assembly that could be dragged around by a truck by its tow fork, with a solar charger mounted on the front, used at night for construction projects. The moth's dance flickered shadows in the little areas where light seemed to reach.

"I'm sorry—what?" Mason asked in disbelief.

"I want to see the zombies," Heather exclaimed in a whisper. "I want to see what they're like."

Mason was shocked. "But you already know what they're like. They're scary, they're dead, and they eat people."

"Not like that," she replied. "I mean, I know what they're like; I just never get to see them up close and actually look at them. Usually, if they were around, we were hiding or running, and we haven't exactly been out at night where we could see them and not get killed."

Mason groaned and replied, "I've seen enough of them."

"Come on," she said defiantly then dragged him to his feet.

"Fine. This ground sucks anyways." Mason trudged behind her toward the aisle end-cap and to the right, toward the side of the enclave with the zombie pens. Once they made their way past the light, they had to stop and let their eyes adjust to the darkness. Aside from the occasional small work light on the end of an extension cord, the place was almost pitch black. There were lights near the aisles and a large room near the ceiling back by the far rear wall; it had windows on three sides, angled so someone could sit in it and peer down at the guards below, but even that seemed empty right then. Most people must have been outside pulling a guard shift or making sure the zombies were secure. The gray outlines of shelves with various items protruding at different angles made their dimensions look warped, like the bows of ghost ships jutting up out of a shadowy sea.

Mason checked to see if the pencil was still in his pocket. Heather pushed forward toward the pens until finally they were standing before a bright light near a chain link fence. After a minute, they realized it was an old Coleman lantern perched on top of a dusty ice chest.

"What do yoo wah't?" Jed asked in a tone that croaked out of the darkness behind them. Both kids spun around to face him, surprised that anyone had snuck up behind them.

Heather couldn't seem to form words, so finally Mason spoke up, "Sh—we wanted to see the zombies you're harvesting."

"No place for children!" Jed snapped. His voice reminded Mason of an angry crocodile.

Near the pens, a voice rang out, "That's fine, Jed, just fine," Dan said in a comforting tone. "Just a natural curiosity. Completely harmless."

Still adamant, Jed repeated, "No place for children!"

A man standing to Jed's left walked up, wearing a light-green overcoat whose sleeves had been very visibly ripped off. "We'll handle it, old man. Go check the front gate."

Jed looked visibly annoyed and finally reached down, picked up a rifle that had been sitting behind the cooler, and turned to walk off into the darkness.

"What do you think, Jenkins?" Dan asked. "Should we let them see the zombies?"

Jenkins smiled as two more men joined them. One, carrying an old Russian AK-47, said, "Better to educate them young," in a sinister voice.

Jenkins perked up and said, "Don't you think we could make better money off them from Falling Sa—" and was sharply cut off as Dan smacked him in the arm with the buttstock of his rifle.

"That ain't our business. Plus, our numbers been down, and they're expecting a shipment down the route," Dan said curtly. "Right this way, children, and watch your step." Dan motioned them through a gate into the zombie pens.

The smell of death was overpowering, as though someone had been burning pork and tires. Mason retched for a moment while Heather just kept walking ahead with a curious look on her face. Dan looked down and noticed Mason retching as he strode past. An evil grin crept across his lips. Mason felt confused and sick to his stomach. He wished Heather had seen the grin, but she was too far ahead to have noticed it. The other men just shuffled up behind Mason.

Cages made of chain link lined one side of the walkway here. The chain link didn't look terribly strong, but the poles on the end of each pen were steel and went directly into the cement. Each cage had a matching chain link gate on the far side of the fence. The cages seemed to push back at least fifty feet into the darkness, although their actual depth was out of sight. On the other side of the walkway began the dusty shelves that led into the rest of the warehouse. They were cluttered full of so many odds and ends they seemed to be almost impenetrable.

As if sensing his concern, Dan looked back and said, "The fence holds. So long as we keep them fairly weak and underfed, they can't break through it. Don't think they don't try, though."

The first caged-off area seemed empty. "We usually house Poisoners in there." Dan drew a breath that sounded like he was feigning concern. "Not often, though; they are pretty dangerous to manage. They emit a paralyzing gas unless starved, and it's hard to tell when they're starved, so it has turned out rather bad for some of our men." Dan just shrugged.

As they passed one of the other cages, a shadow seemed to drift forward. At first, it looked like a person coming into focus as the darkness around its features changed from black to pale white while it edged forward into the dim light. It seemed to be having trouble walking. Heather turned her head to face it and stopped walking, also trying to figure out why its gait didn't seem right.

After a few more seconds of the zombie teetering back and forth, Mason realized its feet weren't on the floor. It seemed to be pretend-walking, its limbs flailing loosely as something else seemed to shake it from the neck. Finally, several large brown limbs appeared on all sides as they alternated stepping forward, leaving at least three of them on the floor at all times. The steps were rhythmic and slow and seemed sure-footed, as if guided by some purpose. The legs, which were curved out from the body toward the floor, made the zombie dangling in the middle resemble some sort of marionette. Suddenly, the massive beast lunged forward, its head lolling back then smashing into the chain-link fence. Mason and Heather leapt back a foot. The chain links bent forward a bit as they gave a little bit of space to the massive creature. Its jaws opened up as it hissed and chewed part of the chain-link in an attempt to get to the humans. Finally it halted momentarily, and large six-inch mandibles slowly crept out from its mouth and curled up, pointing at one of the closest men as if anticipating a moment it would be allowed to strike.

Heather gasped in fear. "It's a giant spider!"

One of the men chuckled callously and said, "It's a Shat."

"What's a Shat?" Mason asked in a whisper.

Jenkins was the first to answer, "A zombie so scary that when you see it... you've already done shat yourself." As the last word trailed off, he gave it an inflection that made it sound like a well-deserved punch line. All the men guffawed and laughed at the joke.

Leaving the Shat spitting and hissing at the fence, they continued on. Finally, they reached a large cage at the end of the walkway. Dan had stepped ahead of Heather, and he stopped and turned around to face everyone. Pride beamed off him as he smiled and said, "Now, the Raven is one of God's great creatures."

Heather and Mason both edged forward, trying to focus on the distance, to get a glimpse of what was in the pen. The darkness slowly parted as a creature stepped out. It crept forward with hollow, gaunt eyes and a nose that was larger and almost beak-like. Drool rolled down the sharpened teeth as they flashed in what little light there was. Its elbows pulled in tight to its sides, its arms bent up slightly, and its wrists curled down, giving the hands a claw-like appearance. It resembled some type of dinosaur waiting to strike. Clacking its teeth and keeping the people to its right, it slowly shuffled forward toward the front corner of the pen. Its head tilted various directions, and every so often its eyes would come to rest on them but then flicker away in another direction as though trying to study them without making eye contact.

It halted, clacked its teeth once more, hissed, and then let out an ear-piercing shriek as it rushed forward toward Mason, clearing twenty feet in two leaps. The shadows in the pen erupted as more screeching Ravens leapt out of the darkness to join the attack signaled by the first one. Gnashing teeth and hands pressed up against the cage and tried to shred their way through the tiny spaces. The cage heaved under the massive weight of multiple zombies smashing up against it.

Mason had fallen and was kicking his feet and pushing back at the same time in an attempt to back up. The hillbilly residents of the enclave erupted into another fit of laughter. Finally, after what seemed like an eternity, the Ravens eased back off the fence, clicked their teeth at different intervals, snapped their heads in different directions, letting their eyes study the humans once more, then finally turned and vanished back into the darkness. Shakily, Mason got to his feet and swerved past the men to stand closer to the exit. Heather was pale at this point and looked as though she might pass out. Mason stumbled over his words, trying to both apologize and excuse themselves out of the pens.

Dan raised a hand firmly and silenced him at once. "You see, the problem with Ravens," Dan began, "is that they don't create other Ravens often. They have a tendency to rage in huge numbers and just rip everything apart to feast. So while they're deadly and spectacular in how they kill, their numbers are not as big in the wild." His tone sounded as though he actually appreciated and admired the undead creatures in some sort of sick way. He smiled, continuing on, "So they're worth a pretty penny to the science enclaves if you can capture them and get them alive." In a quick motion, he grabbed Heather by her arm and spun her around so he was holding her by her neck and facing the other men. Mason gasped and struggled to catch his breath as Heather let out a loud scream, and the pen stirred back to life.

Two of the men moved toward the gate of the compound as the Ravens surged forward to press up against the fence that Heather was near. Dan pressed her face closer to the shrieking and teeth-gnashing wall of undead flesh that was separated by the thin chain-link fence. Just as she was close enough to feel their rasping on her skin, Dan leaned in and whispered, barely loud enough for Mason to hear, "Of course, they need to feed."

In a sudden motion, he lunged toward the gate as the two men snapped it open slightly and helped shove her through. Her screams echoed off the walls of the enclave as the men tried to force the gate closed and avoid being bitten by the mass of undead that surged forward. One man finally managed to get the last zombie to pull its arm back inside the pen by striking it twice with the stock of his rifle. Panting for a moment, they all half chuckled as Heather's screams turned to gasps and then faded to chewing and the sloshing of teeth, followed by the delighted chirps of the Ravens.

All at once, every man looked up at Mason, who was still standing trembling in the darkness. Realizing he had to move, he forced himself to spin, still off balance, and tried to run. Two steps later, he smashed face-first into an older man's chest.

Jed looked down past him with a stone face, not wanting to make eye contact. "I told you this was no place for children," he groaned as he took hold of one of Mason's arms, dragged him kicking and screaming past the hissing Shat, and shoved him into the empty Poisoner cage, locking the gate behind him.

8.

Open World

Zombie Civil Rights Group

Present Day

"ARE YOU ALMOST DONE?" Ashley asked impatiently.

Mason looked up from his work for a moment to acknowledge her, then went back to his painting while muttering, "Rockpotamus hurries for no man."

Donathan laughed slightly behind the two of them. Ashley was not in the mood. "That's it?" she said in a frustrated tone.

Mason stood back for a moment to take in his work. A cartoon hippo painted onto a large boulder stared back at him. "That's it." Dabbing one last patch of purple paint, he repeated, "That's it."

"Not your best work, is it?" she stated bluntly and then turned away from the boulder toward Donathan. Mason just silently agreed with her as he picked up his paint bottles. He had lacked inspiration for the last day or so, and when Donathan had actually told him he could go ahead, all he could think to paint was a hippopotamus.

They stayed the night in the town in a small make-shift boarding room over the general store. Although the town was quiet and the townspeople seemed friendly, the ZCR had cycled out, having one person stay up for two and a half hours while the others slept. Of course, Mason had fallen back asleep as soon as his shift started. That was just a constant with him.

Shortly after dawn broke, they left. Low on cash and supplies, they could only afford a light meal before they set out to find the Ravens. None of the townspeople had ever heard of a Jessica Pulse or a "Princess Jae." Another dead-end. After the job was done, they'd just keep moving toward Half Moon Bay as planned.

Eli had informed them that the nest was only a couple of hours into the foothills above the town, near an old farmstead. The nest was dangerously close to the townspeople, and they had suffered for years because of it, but the only real option was to build their town walls taller and stock their night guards with more ammunition.

As the hills changed from dust and yellow patches of earth, they saw what Eli had meant a few days before when he said the land was fertile. The green covering the hills here flowed down into a valley. Deep, lush pockets of vegetation could be seen in all directions as they neared the farm.

They noticed the old barn as they approached. Faded red wooden shingles and wooden planks looked dull and worn in the morning sun. An old whitewashed farmhouse stood behind it, with a porch sectioned off and surrounded by a bug screen with holes ripped through it. Parts of the roof sagged unnaturally, and they could see old farm equipment rusting in the spot it had come to rest when the undead first arrived. Grass crept up higher around the various old tractors, pitchforks, shovels, and baler equipment, which had been left to the elements.

"The land that time forgot," Mason said as they approached.

Rounding the edge of the barn, Donathan noticed a large elm tree on the horizon past the building. They trudged across the field for a few minutes, approaching it, then Donathan stopped, turned toward his friends, and used sign language.

"Eli says that's where the monsters are," he signed, pointed at the elm tree, then continued, "A cave under the ridge near that tree. From here on, we use sign to keep quiet."

Ashley signed back, "I thought Ravens were only nocturnal."

Donathan nodded and signed, "Yes, but like most, they can still be disturbed and coaxed into the daylight. Better safe than sorry."

Coming up with the plan, Donathan signed that they had better approach from the north side and that Mason could get over to the hilltop near the ridge and begin firing to try to get their attention. As they came rushing out toward the sound of his gun, Donathan and Ashley would fire as much as they could to take down any that emerged from the nest.

Donathan finished with, "If we have to, I'll throw our two firebombs into the nest, but I'd rather not since we only have two for emergency situations. If the nest is too big, we might need them to get away. The contingency plan is to fall back to the farmhouse and hope we can make a good stand."

Mason nodded and signed something strange with the crook of one finger against his cheek.

Donathan and Ashley both looked at him, confused.

He arched one of his eyebrows then performed the same sign again.

Ashley looked at Donathan, then finally back to Mason and said out loud in a stunned voice, "What do you mean, 'I sex'?"

"I understand!" he exclaimed and signed it again with force.

"No, dummy, that's 'I sex'; 'I understand' is this." She then did the sign for "I know."

Mason, frustrated with her, said, "No, it's—" but then waved a hand to cut off the communication as Donathan shushed them both. They all looked toward the sky and listened, trying to identify what they were hearing. It was a low hum, and it seemed to be getting louder. Finally Ashley pointed toward the elm tree. One body was sprinting full speed past the ridge and toward the field they were standing in.

Mason laughed and said, "One zombie? Hell of a nest." Suddenly, the hum increased tenfold as the whole horizon behind the zombie darkened. Bodies were everywhere, rushing toward them. The undead formed a gigantic dark mass of movement loping across the land in their direction.

"Fast movers! *Fast movers!*" Ashley called out as they backed up and fired their weapons into the crowd.

Mason tripped and fell, then scrambled to his feet, running back to find a position to perch his machine gun for the attack. Turning back around, he saw an actual look of determination on Donathan's face. His smile was gone. This was bad.

"Get to the barn!" Donathan screamed over the roar of sound. He hadn't even bothered to put his headphones on. Their element of surprise was gone, and this certainly wasn't going to be a strategic plan, so he thought, Why bother? They made it to one of the barn walls next to an ancient ladder just as the Swarm reached them. Their guns rang out as if trying to shatter the loud, rhythmic sound coming from the undead approaching them. As they formed a semicircle with their backs toward the barn wall, they continued to fire. The zombies were at close range. Donathan had thrown down his rifle and drawn his pistols, and Ashley reached back to unsheathe her bat.

"Get the gun to high ground," Donathan called to Mason, motioning to the ladder.

Mason knew immediately he was right. If they were to stand a chance against this horde, they had to move the gun to a position where it could engage everything. The other two guarded the base of the ladder as Mason ascended. Halfway up, Donathan shouted to his back, "They're not Ravens... They're Swarm!"

People often mistook Ravens for Swarm. They both worked in large groups and were attracted to loud noises. Swarm were a bit different, though. They weren't called Swarm because of their massive numbers, even though they often had huge hives. They weren't called Swarm because of their uncanny ability to hear and move on prey in a unified, chaotic rampage. They were called Swarm because of the massive amounts of flies that would fill their ocular cavities and because of the fluid that dripped down from them, forming veins of blackened, moving masses that trailed down their faces. Most zombies had partial sight, and the other senses were a bit more instinctual. Swarm were totally blind, relying on other senses that had almost become supernatural. Often they would hear, roar to life, and begin attacking people—who had no idea they'd even stumbled into their territory—long before they heard that hum that accompanied Swarm, which could come from the undead themselves or the accumulation of flies caked around their faces. No one knew for sure. They were more opportunistic than any other kind of zombie. Most others refused to attack in sunlight unless provoked because the light seemed to daze or blind them. It was usually the only opportunity for hunters to decimate a hive. Mankind's last failsafe was usually the morning sun. If one could find shelter and live through the night, one might be able to make it. With variants like Swarm, one just hoped to live.

Without time to put their headphones on and coordinate the attack, Donathan and Ashley were improvising.

"I need more room, Ash!" Donathan shouted as he stepped back, firing rounds from one pistol and trying to take in their surroundings. Already zombies had begun scaling the barn in an attempt to chase after Mason. Swarm didn't really need ladders here; flesh ripped and tore as they cleaved makeshift holes into the half-rotten wooden walls of the barn. Other denizens of the horde scaled overhead by grabbing onto the holes or other undead and anything else to climb up after their prey. The sweet sickly scent of the horde hung in the air, a smell like a mixture of honey and dead flesh.

Ashley's bat found the beat, and the world erupted around her. She stepped back and swung forward, the bat sailing ahead in her right hand as her stance widened out, her hips rotating to push power into the blunt swing. As the bat arced forward, her wrist turned inward, increasing the power of the swing. The bat connected with the head of one of the undead, causing bits of flesh, brain matter, and flies to scatter everywhere. The crack of bone and aluminum rang out. Even before the undead fell to the ground, she had spun around, letting the momentum of the spin carry the bat in the opposite direction toward another Swarm. The bat collapsed part of its face, then she turned to let the bat swing down and forward to hammer the ankle of another undead, sweeping it out from under it and causing it to topple into the other creatures rushing forward. A look of determination and focus crossed her face as she opened her mouth slightly to exhale and continue her assault. She had definitely settled into the rhythm of the moment.

Donathan saw the space Ashley had cleared and felt the music cue him in as he lowered his head and surged forward. He felt the world slow around him as the undead's actions seemed to hang for a second with each pulse of speed. His boot connected with an undead chest as his pistols rang to life. Each time one of his rounds impacted an undead, the flies on its face would scatter for a moment and reconvene in similar spots as the corpse fell to the ground with a fresh bullet hole in the skull. Dodging past clawing hands and snapping mouths had become second nature by then. Occasionally he would miss and have to fire a second shot at the creature, but even reloading came easily as the world almost ground to a halt. He knew that if he paused even for a second to draw a deeper breath or study the trajectory of one of the falling creatures, he would lose the beat, and the moment would be lost. Ignoring how exhausted and overwhelmed they were, he was propelled forward by one thought: If Mason could get the gun up, they might just survive.

The higher Mason climbed, the more the wooden ladder swayed. The machine gun was slung behind him with the strap partially across his right shoulder and pulling on the front of his neck. It felt like an anchor as he forced his limbs to continue working as hell erupted below. The thuk thuk sound of his feet on the wooden rungs, combined with the loud hum of the undead, the ping of an aluminum bat, and the crack of pistols firing below, began to create a slight beat. Mason felt the music rush into existence as he reached the top of the barn. Heaving the machine gun forward, he scrambled up onto the old wooden roof and gasped a second before half-running toward the front, intending to position the gun to fire down into the mob of bodies below. As he reached the middle of the roof, he halted. Bodies had already begun scrambling up over the edge and onto the roof.

Spinning around, Mason tried to take in what he was seeing. Scattered undead stood up near the edges and formed a perimeter around him. The horizon darkened as boards creaked and shuddered. "Guys..." Mason spoke to the zombies shuffling in a circle around him and stalking their prey. "This is pretty dangerous," he added in a meager attempt to reason with the undead. Reaching up, he slowly pulled down his mask to reveal, written in calm letters, the words "Don't Panic"—except he had scratched out the word "Don't" with a series of frustrated lines forming an angry X mark.

Suddenly, one of the Swarm off to his left flexed its arms out and fashioned its rotting hands into fists. Straightening its arms, it swung its head forward and screamed. Others around it joined the fray, screaming a raspy, guttural roar at Mason as their bodies tensed. The flies, which had formed black masses across their eyes and pulsing black veins that hung down under the faces of the living corpses, scattered and buzzed in the air. The hollow eyes and graying flesh came into view as the creatures continued screaming and baring their teeth in hungry rage. Finally, all the screams died back into the hum as the collective undead on the rooftop all sprinted toward Mason. Wood snapped and buckled all around as the roof collapsed and Mason fell screaming into the darkness below.

At the base of the building, Ashley heard his screams and lost the beat. Her bat failed to connect as panic took over, and her own scream of "No!" sprang up just as Mason's died off. Donathan picked up the slack, but it was clear they were losing the fight as they eased their backs closer to the barn wall. What little space they had created seemed to be fading away as corpses shuffled forward.

"No!" Ashley screamed again in a voice full of fear and sadness.

"Yes!" an excited voice echoed back.

"No..." Ashley screamed, almost sobbing as she fell back against the barn.

"Yes! Yes! YES!" came an excited scream from the barn.

Swinging her bat forward one last time, Ashley shouted out, confused, "Yes?"

The front side of the barn seemed to explode as old wood shattered and splintered everywhere, creating a cloud of dust, and a green wheat-harvesting combine smashed through. The blades on the front of the combine spun with a blur in the morning sunlight.

The beat of the moment changed. The horde turned its attention to the loudest thing there. Being blind, they could hear only the combine's roar. The undead quickly ran or shuffled away from Donathan and Ashley.

Mason perched on a seat atop the machine and spun the steering wheel, turning the combine around in the field as the first zombies smashed head-on into the blades. Necrotic flesh and bone rained down as Mason laughed and shouted, *"Un-limit-ed power!"*

Ashley lowered her bat and stared, stunned for a moment, as a huge mass of the undead sprinted head-on into the blades. The combine shuddered slightly as it charged forward, showering the land with body parts. When Mason set his machine gun on a metal platform just in front of his seat and fired on the remaining horde as he spun the wheel with his other hand, she finally grimaced and muttered, "Overachiever."

Donathan just redonned his usual stone smile and pulsed forward toward the remaining zombies, shouting for Ashley to follow suit. Gunfire and spinning blades drowned out the hum as the last of the horde were struck down.

Off in the distance, one lone zombie ran back toward the elm tree, screaming as it did so. Ashley shouted up to

Mason, "Hey, dummy, if he gets away, then the—"

Mason was already firing down on it. A loud burst of gunfire erupted as the final undead was ripped in half by a wall of gunfire.

Looking down at his friends, Mason just laughed and asked, "You were saying?"

Just then the ground shook violently. The elm tree fell over, and a cloud of dirt appeared as a large silhouette charged up, out of the ground, and toward the friends.

"QUEEN!" Donathan shouted as he motioned to the house for their fallback point. Mason did a double take at the queen. It was a large mass of flesh that ran hunched over, its muscled arms sprawled ahead of it, dragging its person-sized knuckles along the ground. Its massive, hollow eyes were filled with pools of flies and dark veins that seemed to spread off its face down most of its body, shifting and skittering as it ran. Most of its oversized bulk was arms and a head, so it had a tendency to lean forward as it rushed toward them. For a moment, Mason considered crashing the combine into it, but it proved its legs weren't just for aesthetic purposes by leaping high into the sky. Swearing, Mason grabbed his machine gun with two hands and dove off the combine just as the Queen came smashing down onto it. The metal machine warped and pitched as the weight of the Queen destroyed it. Gigantic jaws and sharp fangs snapped at Mason's departure as it struggled to regain its balance and continue its pursuit.

Crossing the front porch's threshold and diving into the house, Mason slammed the door with force, turned to one of the windows to set up his machine gun, and began to rain lead hell down on the oversized beast when Donathan grabbed his arm and in a determined voice warned, "Don't."

Looking around the living room, Mason noticed tubes, funnels, glass beakers, gas cans and unlit Bunsen burners. Labels of duct tape and faded writing from permanent markers donned the various pieces of equipment that seemed to be everywhere. Finally Mason asked, "Is this a science enclave?"

Ashley half laughed while feigning humor; clearly the situation was getting to her. "More like an ancient meth lab."

Mason panicked and said, "Let's get out of here," then tried to open the front door and saw the creature rushing toward the house, dragging part of the combine tractor behind it. Frustrated, it snapped its jaws as Mason closed the door, saying, "Forgot."

Everyone scrambled toward the back of the house and kicked out the kitchen window. One after another they each dove through and sprinted back toward the nearest foothill. When they got about twenty yards away, Donathan stopped, took his pack off his back, and unpacked the two petrol bombs.

Producing a Zippo lighter with the faded graphic of a parachute with a set of wings on it, he flicked the top and produced a flame, lighting up the cloth extending from the glass bottles, and let it cake the top halves in flame. Ashley had already returned to his side as Mason continued sprinting toward the hill. She held out her hand as if expecting a Christmas present. Taking hold of the bottle, she sneered wickedly as she drew her foot back and threw her shoulder forward, arcing the bottle across the open space toward the house. Donathan did the same. The first bottle smashed the roof, spreading flaming petrol across the ruined wooden shingles. The second bottle smashed into the back of the house, igniting the wall and the window frame they recently exited. Suddenly, the whole back wall of the house ripped open as the queen smashed through, raising its head to the sky and ignoring the flaming ground and wall it had just pushed through. Its scream carried death and pain across the barren wind for a moment before the house made a slight popping sound. The beast stopped screaming and looked back and down for a moment while a confused look crossed its fly-covered face. The house vanished in a loud explosion that sent flame, wood, and rotten flesh in all directions.

9.

Rift Parish

Mason

Five Years Earlier

"THEY'VE VANISHED," Jenkins said to Dan in a tone of frustration. "You don't think they found a way out—"

"What 'out' would that be, Jenkins?" Dan replied with an annoyed voice. Jenkins just shrugged as Dan added, "They're hiding. Start checking the shelves, or..." Drawing in a breath, he said, "Let's just expand the pens when we're done with the little one here." From the back of the dark cage, Mason could see Dan motioning to him.

The cage was empty, except for some severed and stripped bone, dirt on the concrete, and a small throw rug that smelled like hair, earth, and copper.

From around the aisle corner limped a man with white hair. "Complications?" Aaron asked in a dry voice.

"Just tying up loose ends," Dan replied. "Can you give the order to move most of the men topside and to the garden area? We're gonna expand."

Aaron blinked for a moment, drew a breath, and said scornfully, "This whole night was a terrible idea. These people are—"

"Are what put food on the table. They're why we have electricity and gas and ammunition. I've got everything under control, Dad." Dan wasn't about to let Aaron tell him he was wrong.

Aaron let his judgmental gaze rest on Dan's weathered face for another minute before making a frustrated *harumph* and walking back around the corner.

Waving his men forward, Dan moved toward the gate of Mason's cage. Sensing his only opportunity, Mason stepped forward out of the darkness into the light and toward his only exit. Dan just smiled as the men edged toward the gate, lumbering something forward that they kept gripped tightly, yet somehow still extending their arms to keep it a fair ways away as it struggled between them. The three oversized men seemed to be having issues pulling it along. Mason already knew what it was before Dan snapped open the gate to let them shove it in.

Mason thought about climbing the fence to get to a higher point, but each cage had razor wire lining the top. He thought about backing away into the darkness, but at the time, he couldn't force his limbs to respond. There only seemed to be enough time to draw breath, and then, standing in front of him, clicking its teeth and darting its eyes back and forth at its surroundings, was a Raven.

It was a man, only slightly taller than Mason. Looking malnourished and skinny, his dark eyes were hollow, and his nose was more elongated and sharper than a normal person's. Its clothes were a torn red t-shirt and tight jeans. It actually still had one white tennis shoe, but the other foot was bare and even had some flesh missing from the top near its ankle. It didn't seem to notice Mason.

"Remember how I said Ravens don't seem to infect others?" Dan asked. The Raven hissed and turned away from Mason toward the fence the moment Dan had begun speaking. "Not when they're by themselves." The elation in Dan's voice was increasing. "You'll fetch a pretty penny from the science enclaves when this is all over."

Laughing in a vindictive manner, Jenkins turned toward the fence near Dan, letting his rifle drift down to his side, "Who knows? Maybe they'll save you."

More hillbillies seemed to join the camaraderie as they walked up to surround the front of the cage, and one exclaimed, "Maybe you'll save the world." They all burst into laughter, which caused the Raven to hiss and rush the fence, snapping at the chortling men. None of them even seemed to notice. After a minute, they all got quiet and waited for the zombie to spy its victim.

Mason's heart hurt as it beat in his chest. He could hear the blood in his ears. His head felt cold and dizzy as the world turned gray around him. He just wished the moment was over already, wished for the life of peace and modern amenities that he had known once, before the whole apocalypse—video games his father spoke of, movie theatres, whole conventions where they actually sold comics and shook hands with movie stars, directors, and authors. Life must have been amazing once.

The Raven turned to face Mason, its teeth clicking as it did. Its head snapped into place as its eyes slowed their darting and came to rest where Mason was.

Without breathing, Mason slowly hunched over and raised one arm up in a bent form, which caused the Raven to hiss and draw back one of its feet. Then Mason turned and shook and shuffled his feet across the cage in a mechanical fashion. His head moved in a circular motion as his arms and legs clicked on, marching in a synchronized path as he did his best to imitate a wind-up toy, with terrible posture, crossed with a monkey of some kind. Once he reached the edge of the cage, he turned, his mind screaming, and forced himself to march back toward the other side of the cage while making tick tick clack whir noises over and over. He did this for a good thirty seconds before the zombie grunted.

Figuring the end was near, Mason stopped his latest march across the cage and turned to face the undead while stopping his wind-up noises. Grunting again, the zombie shivered as if it were in pain. Then all at once, it seemed to gag and spasm. After a second, Mason realized it was laughing. He had somehow succeeded in making a zombie laugh.

The men around the cage looked stunned. Even Mason stood up a little straighter, trying to figure out what to do next, a look of shock on his face. Finally, after an eternity of the zombie's wheezing and sputtering chuckles, the men around the cage laughed too. Everyone seemed to be enjoying themselves. Mason got a bit comfortable and laughed too, just to fit in with all the others around him.

The Raven's head swayed up and down as it panted and laughed. Mason heard one melodic tone ring out in his head as he sprinted with full force toward the front of the cage and tackled the zombie. The second the undead's head bounced off the floor, Mason was already bringing down his clenched hand, hammering the Raven across the face with the bottom of his fist. He continued smashing the undead's face violently until it went limp.

Sitting back and taking a moment to really see what he'd done, Mason noticed the Raven's nose had been smashed straight back into its face. It hadn't taken much force or many swings, but it seemed to have killed the creature almost instantly.

"Son of a bitch!" Dan shouted with rage. "We try to cash in for another, and we're down one now. Get him out." He waved his hand toward Mason in a way that made the other men leap into action. Dan patted his pants frantically, searching for something, until he produced a small dip canister. By the time he had it open and was shoveling tobacco into his mouth, Mason was already being dragged out of the cage.

"Stand him up over there." On Dan's command, Jenkins motioned with his rifle for Mason to stand in the middle of the aisle next to the cage.

After backing up, each man carefully kept his weapon pointed in Mason's direction and watched him.

After settling the can back in his pocket, Dan said, "Take aim."

The men changed their stance from just aiming at Mason to a controlled stance in which their legs drew back while each man raised his weapon slightly to make sure they were looking down the iron sights at their target.

"Wai-wai-wai-wait!" Mason shouted in a panic. "One question. Just one quick question."

Dan looked curious, so he spat once and then said, "Go ahead."

Mason looked down and ground the toe of one of his sneakers into the floor while asking, "If...uhh...If award-winning actor Jack Nicholson was stuck on a domesticated horse, would you help Jack off a domesticated horse?"

All of the men looked puzzled. Finally, the man in the front lowered his weapon and said, "Well... yeah." Then he cleared his throat and added, "I remember his movies... I would."

Cutting him off, another man lowered his weapon and said, "Well, he won the Oscar, so yeah, I'd help."

Finally, Dan became annoyed at the fact that all his men had lost sight of what was going on, so he said curtly, "Yes, yes, we'd all help jack off a horse."

Each man looked confused as Dan said this. One looked down and away, another looked up toward the roof, and another just got a distant stare in his eyes. Dan lowered his head entirely, shaking it and cursing himself.

Mason turned to his right and ran full speed at the dusty, oversized shelf filled with items and dove into it.

10.

Goodbye from the Edge of Never

Hunter S. Thompson

Twenty Years Earlier

IT HAD BEEN A SLOW WEEK. Frank, next door, had been eaten on Friday by the zombie invasion. It wasn't a terrible loss, since he had borrowed my mower and never given it back, but he was always steady on poker night, so it was definitely a bother. Ken and his wife April, up the street, had fled somewhere north with a station wagon packed full of belongings and supplies. I suppose it's for the best, since they had a little one, but I still can't get over the fact they used to bring the best damn snacks for our weekly poker game. Then, of course, there's Martin. He actually didn't get eaten or flee the apocalypse. The guy is just an asshole, so I stopped inviting him.

Anyways, it was pushing Thursday evening about five when the idea finally struck me. I had the news on, not because I like hearing about the one billion reported dead or missing as the dead come back to life, but because Jeopardy was canceled, and this was all that was on. I guess zombies have no use for "The name of this channel can be traced back to a movie theater that opened in 1905 in McKeesport, PA." I don't know either, so it's just as well. I had heard some shuffling around my front porch, so I opened the door, and standing before me, swaying slightly and making a slight gurgling sound, was one of the undead. I was frightened for the first ten seconds, then I noticed he was wearing a small black vest and the tattered remains of matching slacks. His glasses were crooked on his face, and one of the lenses had been smashed back into his eye, obviously from a prior engagement with a survivor that hadn't turned out quite as planned. Here was a stately fellow who had obviously come for my poker game.

"Come in, good sir, come in," I said as I rushed him to his seat at my card table in the other room. I shoved and sat him down rather roughly in the chair despite his protests and sat across from him while sorting the chips and offering him a beer that I had set out in an ice chest next to the table many hours before.

"Beer, sir?" I asked as he continued to ignore my offer and just twitch in the chair while letting his eyes dart from left to right as if taking in his new surroundings and protesting them at the same time. Setting the beer back down, I shuffled and dealt the cards.

"Really is a good day for a card game, don't you think? I mean the weather's just been absolute trash." I had already slid his two cards over and dealt two cards to myself when I turned over the flop to reveal the ace of spades, the four of diamonds, and the ace of clubs. Turning over my hand, I noticed I had the ace of hearts and the two of diamonds.

What an excellent hand. Three of a kind with the potential for the nuts of four of a kind. Spectacular.

The zombie hadn't even looked at his hand. After a few minutes of watching him gurgle, then shift and stare past me at my back window, I became frustrated, "Sir, you haven't even looked at your cards. This is poker. We need to bet, so I'm going to go ahead and throw in your chips and call mine." Doing just that, I burnt a card to the bottom of the deck and flipped over the turn card, sliding it next to the flop. Nine of spades. That certainly didn't help me. But I could bluff this son of a bitch out; after all he was just a zombie. I shoved some chips in the pot and announced, "Raise you thirty."

The zombie made a disgusting sound as part of his cheek fell off onto the table.

"For Christ's sake, HANDLE YOUR SHIT, man. This is twenty-year-old felt from a collectible table I picked up cheap... at a flea market. I mean, this could possibly be a collectible table, and now it's got...wait, what is that?" I was stunned for a moment. "Green blood? You have green blood? You need to get that checked. I'm pretty thankful you didn't have that beer now. Who knows what sort of interaction that could have caused?" The zombie leaned back and wheezed loudly then ended the sound with a frustrated grunt as one of his arms spasmed toward me in a grabbing motion.

I went ahead and slid his call into the pot. There's no way I was going to wait to see what his cards were when he clearly wasn't as stately as I had originally thought. Turning over the river card revealed the two of hearts. YES! I had a FULL HOUSE! Cathedral bells and loud gongs went off in my head as trumpets seemed to sound in every nerve in my body. I had to maintain my composure, so I drew in a breath slowly then double-checked the cards to try to feign weakness before sliding a moderate bet into the pot.

The zombie lolled his head forward and retched, but luckily, nothing came up.

In a friendly tone I added, "Good man there, zombie. Looking out for the felt like I asked. I'm gonna go ahead and slide your bet in." Reaching under his hands, I grasped his chips and then turned over his cards. "So let's just see what you have." Smiling because I had a full house, I announced loudly, "Ace of hearts and an ace of spades. Well done, zombie, but I think I..." I realized something was wrong as the zombie made a squealing sound across from me and struggled in his chair. I looked at the cards again. "Wait a minute. That's five aces."

The zombie turned toward me, let his eyes come to rest on mine, and hissed loudly, slowly letting his face creep forward across the table.

"Why, you cheating son of a bitch!" I yelled. "How dare you come into my house, bleed green on my green felt, and then cheat at cards." By this point, the zombie had stood up, toppling the table. I slid out of my chair and, still shouting over his hissing and spitting, announced, "I believe I'm going to have to ask you to leave."

The zombie closed just one of his eyes then leaned forward, placing a foot on the toppled cards and chips that lay strewn everywhere. He shrugged his shoulders and edged his arms up to his side, his stance resembling an angry tiger prepared to strike. He let out a loud shriek that finally tapered off, and the whole house became silent as if preparing for his next move.

"Damned sorry about all of this, friend. I get a little competitive," the zombie said.

"Holy shit, a talking zombie!" I shouted.

11.

Bantam Town

Zombie Civil Rights Group

Present Day

"A TIME MACHINE!" Mason exclaimed.

Donathan actually looked confused for a moment, but it was Ashley who asked first, "You want to make a time machine?"

Mason nodded as they passed more houses in the town. "A time machine. It needs to have a way to travel, a clock, because all time machines need time," his voice got more enthusiastic and obsessive as his sentence continued, "and a mystical element that makes time travel possible, like a flux capacitor." He was practically hyperventilating.

"But it doesn't have to work?" questioned Ashley.

Mason shook his head and said, "No—"

"Kind of like the Puppy Suit!" she interjected.

Stopping midstep, Mason turned to her and argued the merits of the Puppy Suit as Ashley argued back. Fiery words were exchanged as the street filled with rage. Donathan tried to smooth things over by reasoning and taking control so the argument would stop, but he only managed to make things worse. They all stood only a few feet apart in a circle, bickering until a pop rang out.

Donathan shushed them all and asked, "Do you hear that?" For a long moment, all they could hear was silence.

Ashley looked around and asked, "Where is everyone?"

A hiss was followed by another pop, and the three dropped their packs and sprinted to cover. Ashley and Mason wound up on one side of the street while Donathan was on the other. Waving a hand across to them, Donathan signed the number six, followed by eight. Ashley noticed it first and mimicked him. Mason, standing behind her, finally noticed and also imitated the sign. They were all in sync. When Donathan nodded, they all reached down and cued up a track on their mp3 players labeled "Doomtree - Beacon."

Donathan signed for Mason to go high and for Ashley to be prepared. Mason disappeared into one of the doorways and sprinted up a set of stairs behind Ash as she huddled up against the wall, holding her rifle.

"Those were warning shots. Throw out your weapons," said someone up the street.

Donathan nodded to Ashley, who threw her rifle into the center of the street but kept her bat on her back. Donathan threw out his pistols.

"Now come out," the deep voice commanded.

Ashley turned first and hesitantly stepped out. The music was blaring in her ears, but she still hadn't found the beat. Her feet kicked up dust in the afternoon sun as she stepped up the street with a sour look on her face. Once she had made it a few strides ahead, Donathan sauntered out, bearing a malicious grin.

Dark triangular eyes, rifles, and grilled breathing apparatuses of two men aimed back at them from up the street. Eli stood next to them in his brown trousers, with his hands handcuffed and his head lowered.

Once Ash had made it halfway up the street, a man called out to them, "By order of the Protectorate Army, the members of the ZCR are now under arrest. It will be determined at a later date whether or not you deserve rights. Flee, and you will be executed." The soldier's helmet bobbed as he was calling out these orders. He had made sure to pronounce "ZCR" with an air of contempt. When he was done speaking, he nodded to the second man, who lowered his rifle to waist height and ran down the street toward them while pawing at his waistband for handcuffs. On his tenth step, the beat dropped in.

Ashley flexed her ankle and extended her step, letting her momentum roll forward. Determination flooded her movements as her shoulders squared toward the soldier, and her gait extended into a sprint. The man fumbled for his rifle while trying to raise the weapon. A wicked grin flashed across her face, and she arched backward, letting her body flow into a slide between the man's armor-clad legs. The hip-hop song's chorus sounded in her ear, letting the world come into focus, and she reached up, taking hold of the buttstock and letting her body drift through. In one quick moment, she had completely wrenched the rifle from the soldier's hands. Spinning onto her belly, she tucked the rifle's buttstock next to her hip and then sprang up to a knee, facing the man she'd just disarmed. As the round exited the chamber, Donathan surged past her. With a flash and a thump, she knew that the bullet had hit its mark. She let the next beat sound as she leapt to her feet, spinning, swinging, and throwing the rifle forward ahead of her.

The song crescendoed as the rifle spun through the air toward its mark. Sunlight flickered off of the wood-grain stock as it rotated through the sky. One hand reached up and snatched it out of the air, then pointed it back toward Ashley as the beat kicked back in and she blinked back in a dazed fashion. The first soldier had let his gun fall, leaving it hanging by its weapon sling, and he had run and intercepted the thrown rifle.

She drew a breath as he took aim at her through the iron sights.

Crimson sprayed everywhere as Donathan buried a knife deep into the man's neck between the armor plates and his helmet. Eli had already fallen back, staring dumbfounded from where he sat.

Pulling the earbuds from his ear, Donathan flicked the blood off and sheathed his Bowie knife and remarked to the soldier's trembling mass of flesh in the dirt, "You didn't think I'd have a backup plan?"

One of the alleyways chimed back, "And we wouldn't?"

Turning to his left, Donathan dropped his earbuds. His smile fell away, and shock spread across his face. Out of the corner of his eye, he saw Ashley's head rise as she leaned back from where she was standing with one foot on the other soldier's neck. Finally, out of the alleyway's shadow stepped a third soldier, aiming a rifle steadily at Donathan. After three steps into the sunlight, the man raised his rifle higher and took aim at Donathan's head.

Behind him in a second floor window, Mason waved down to Donathan and gave him a big grin.

Donathan looked past the man and shot an annoyed look at Mason, nudging his head toward the soldier.

Realizing what he should be doing, Mason reached up and lowered his mask to reveal a knight's chess piece, took aim, and fired down into the soldier's back.

After the last round of the burst echoed off into the sky, Mason raised his mask and looked off to his left while disappearing into the room. His excited voice sounded through the window a second later, "Can I have this yarn?"

Eli looked up from the third soldier's body toward the window and said, "Son, you can have anything you want."

"Got any crayons?" Mason yelled back.

12.

Rift Parish

Mason

Five Years Earlier

A MAN WEARING a checkerboard-patterned suit covered with pockets of yapping puppies stared at Mason. Blinking and sniffing, Mason finally looked up from his drawing to survey all his creations. Puppy Suit prototype 7 was complete. Shifting his weight, Mason tucked the pencil back into his pocket and crawled carefully off his left side, away from the shelf covered in drawings, and through the stored collection of junk. He peered down into the warehouse. Below him, the darkness clicked its teeth, and a shadow shifted past the aisle.

An hour before, the men had set up a second set of fencing farther back in the warehouse, leaving only two aisles unfenced below. The fencing stood ten feet in height and had razor-wire strewn across the top of it. At this point, most of the men had given up searching through the mass of items in the aisles below and just spread outside to the perimeter and rooftops, leaving a skeleton crew of a few men inside to search the final aisle's shelving. One brave soul popped open the Ravens' cage and sprinted to the final opening in the fence line as his fellows hooted and laughed at his fear-filled face while he ran through the dusty shadows. Once he'd made it out, the area was secured, and the men just shouted taunts into the dark warehouse as items shifted around. Most of the comments were about how the Ravens would do their job and there was little hope.

Mason had managed to get to the aisle next to the fence's edge and was hidden under the top shelf. Once he had produced his pencil, he had gone to work drawing and lost focus completely on his dangerous situation. The only time he stopped drawing was when loud screams followed by shrieks had echoed behind him from the center of the warehouse. The Ravens had obviously found a victim among his friends who were hiding in one of the other aisles. All he could do as the Ravens swarmed below him was stare at one of his drawings with unfocused eyes and pray for salvation. Eventually, the noise had faded and he had gone back to his art.

He could see moonlight cascading through a few tiny windows at the topmost part of the warehouse's far wall. For a few minutes, Mason stared at them, past the items, trying to figure out if he could somehow find a way through them. Some time passed until he finally concluded that there was nothing high enough on that wall for him to scamper up there and also that even if he could, the windows might be too small or impossible to open. He could always try to make his way up there and then break one. But the noise would most likely draw the guards' attention, and then he'd attract gunfire instead of the undead. The warehouse seemed completely secure, either to keep the night out or the darkness in.

The labyrinth of aisles and items from a world past didn't seem to have any exits save for the front door and the side garden. The front was barricaded shut, and the side garden entrance was guarded by the few men searching the aisle contents below. For the moment, even sound seemed to be halted and silent here.

"Gotcha!" came a shout from below as sounds of pleas mixed with desperation shattered the eerie calm. Mason jolted backward the first moment bright beams illuminated the darkness, convinced he had somehow given away his position, until he realized that the voice begging below belonged to Ethan. Finally, he edged forward, allowing his eyes and forehead to be lit up as he surveyed the scene below.

Three guards had weapons drawn and were pointing them toward the far aisle warehouse corner, exactly the spot they had been given to "rest" when they first arrived. Ethan had just climbed into the shelving unit and surrounded himself and the child with garbage items as camouflage. Ethan and the small girl were right there under their noses. He was clutching the girl under his chest and pleading with the guards with a hand up, begging them for mercy. His voice was a mix of anxiety and sobs as the guard who had found them stood a few feet away, shouting for them to stay where they were. Neither the guard nor Ethan would quiet his voice, and the Ravens hissed and shrieked occasionally, clustering around and facing the onlookers from the other side of the fence. Mason could see them shift and stalk back and forth only a few yards below his hiding hole. His eyes hurt, and his breath felt strained as the scene became louder and more volatile. Finally, a shout seemed to silence everything as a man came in through the garden entryway and limped with a determined strut toward the activity.

Ethan croaked out, "Oh, thank God. Mr. Aaron, sir. Please sir, you didn't want us to stay, and we're sorry we imposed, but this has been—"

"Quiet. Just..." Aaron sighed, then continued in a strained voice, "don't talk." He halted in front of the three men with weapons raised. Aaron drew a deep breath and said, "Just kill them quickly. I've had enough of tonight's nonsense."

Ethan cried out in protest, and the child screamed as the closest guard ripped her from his arms and put her on her knees facing away from him. Producing a pistol from a holster, he took aim just inches from the back of the child's head. Ethan rushed forward to help her, and one of the other guards lunged into him, smashing the buttstock of his rifle into the side of his head and leaving Ethan a crumpled mess of sobbing flesh on the floor.

One lone, ear-piercing shriek rose up from the mob of Ravens below, and suddenly the concrete echoed the sounds of rushing, stomping feet as the fence creaked. Mason's eyes darted directly below him as the Ravens sprinted in circles, bouncing off the fence one at a time as their chaotic mass swarmed together, pulsing forward and backward in an organized movement.

All of the guards backed away from the fence, and one shouted out to Aaron, "What the hell are they doing?"

Finally, one of the Ravens got caught in a tiny seam of the chain link fence, ripped from the constant force of bodies smashing into it. The makeshift fence line heaved as, one after another, the other zombies smashed into the caught one's back, wedging him farther and farther into the fence. Aaron shouted, and one guard sprinted through the garden entrance to warn the others as the remaining guards fired into the Ravens' numbers. In all the fear and shouting, most of the rounds connected with the caught zombie, whose body went from struggling to limp. One of the other undead had fallen and was dragging its injured self away from the group as the rest of the undead became more galvanized. Their surging numbers shuffled faster, and they smashed their bodies into the dead corpse, breaching the fence with such tenacity that its necrotic flesh and bone tore and splintered away until finally, a hole large enough to crawl through had been created. As the guards finally realized they were underpowered and out of ammo, one of the Ravens shuffled through the hole and tried to wrench its caught leg free.

The remaining guards closest to the garden doorway sprinted toward it. Only two of them made it as the third was leapt upon by the Raven and, in a screaming, shrieking moment of fear, had his jugular ripped out, spraying crimson across the floor. The other Ravens clacked their teeth excitedly.

Mason's eyes were drawn to the contents of the top of the aisle behind the men below. A chainsaw's bulky red body almost gleamed in the light. The thin coat of dust on its relatively new-looking frame only seemed to make it glow luminescently as the beams of light shone from below. Mason reached up above him and secured the top shelf, then swung one of his legs up and dragged the rest of his body over the awkward crook above. Pausing to take a quick glance below, he noticed a second Raven had become wedged in the hole while trying to scamper through, and the bloodthirsty collection of zombies had frenzied forward, smashing their bodies into the creature, trying to press past.

Standing up, Mason backed up to the edge of the oversized shelf through one of the few clear paths and let his eyes refocus in the direction of the chainsaw and the center shelves, across the clearing. Looking down, he drew a breath and took a conscious moment to force the trembling from his legs. The rhythm of the zombies' frenzy and heaving of the chain link, combined with the panicked pleas from the captives and the shouts of the alarmed guards outside, created an ethereal sound that echoed across the darkness. Mason heard the melody of words yet unformed as the beat came in.

Tendons lurched, causing his first step to jolt forward. The shelf shook and creaked as the second step slammed down. With the final step planted on the shelf's edge, his entire body shifted up and forward from his sprint across the chasm of puzzled onlookers below. The music crescendoed and halted; he realized for a moment that this rest of his leap was in God's hands. Eyes widening and arms flailing, Mason finally reached out as he smashed into the shelving in front of him. He hadn't leaped high enough and was hanging on to the edge of the two shelving units that had been wedged together to form the aisle. Reaching up, he took a firmer grip on the shelf above him and flailed his legs, trying to find a foothold. Finally catching something, he realized the shelf had shaken unnaturally and looked down to see the toothy, wicked grin of a determined Raven staring up at him from below. Without any razor-wire to impede its ascent, one of the Ravens had taken notice of Mason and begun climbing after him. As it clicked its teeth and reached for one of his legs, Mason looked back up toward the shelf with the chainsaw and climbed. The shelf shook unnaturally again as the undead screeched and dragged itself up after him.

Below Mason, a second Raven had managed to make it through the hole and was standing in the center of the aisle in front of the other humans, effectively blocking their only escape. It clicked its teeth while quickly turning its head in various directions, taking in its surroundings. Its eyes seemed to be edging closer and closer to the remaining survivors. Aaron, still facing the zombie, slowly slid back into the corner toward Ethan and the girl in a final act of self-preservation. His eyes were wide and his limp hardly noticeable for the moment.

The shelf shifted and creaked again as the Raven took hold of one of Mason's legs. Snorting and screeching, it violently tugged on his pant leg, trying to rip him down.

Mason kept his eyes focused on the edge of that top shelf where he could picture that chainsaw staring back at him from the other side. Gripping tightly with his left hand on the metal frame of the other shelf's edge, he extended his right hand skyward toward the shelf where the chainsaw was perched. The chainsaw shifted slightly as the creaking metal and wood made a sudden popping sound. In a final effort to extend his body up toward the top shelf, Mason tensed the leg still planted on the shelf, pushed off against the weight of the zombie, and reached skyward. Finally, his hand reached the height of the top shelf and halted in the air in front of the chainsaw.

His arm wavered as he reached past the chainsaw toward the edge of the next top shelf, where a small paintbrush sat. As people shouted below, the Raven holding Mason's leg shrieked, and the shelf lurched backward a foot, buckling under the weight and then halting for a moment as a splinter of sound and destruction rang out. A small smile spread across Mason's face as he struggled to extend his fingers high enough to reach the tiny blue paintbrush.

Finally, the shelf gave way and began to fall, and Mason felt his inertia shift backward. In a panicked moment, his body fell down a few feet as he reached for the metal frame of the shelf next to the collapsing one and took hold of it with his right hand. Letting his body shift to that side and out of the way of the crumbling metal, wood, and junk that fell past him, he felt his leg lurch free of the Raven, falling below. The entire shelving unit next to his collapsed onto the Ravens in the aisle and the ones behind the fence, crushing them all with several tons of hardware and items from a world before this. Mason let one hand go and dangled, looking down as the chainsaw tumbled into the chaos below and out of sight.

Aaron, Ethan, and the girl all stared up dumbfounded as Mason swung back overhead and climbed again toward the paintbrush's resting spot on the top of the still-standing shelving unit. His right hand reached up to grasp the edge of one of the shelves. Sporting equipment that had shifted in the struggle had come to rest in the same spot his hand was reaching, and instead of a secure wooden plank was the cold, misshapen form of a hockey mask. His eyes widened and his hand gripped it tightly as it slid off the shelf, and Mason fell backward in a split second, realizing his error. Falling downward and pulling the hockey mask toward himself in an act of desperation, he crashed into the items below.

Shocked by what he'd just seen, Ethan tensed as he whispered the word, "Hey." His eyes focused on where Mason's body had disappeared into the dust and junk.

The rubble shifted, and for a moment, a silhouette formed in the shadows and settling dust as someone climbed up out of the wreckage.

Ethan asked nervously, "M-mason?"

The shadow screeched loudly and then clicked its teeth. A Raven stepped forward off the pile of rubble, its arms pulled in tight to its sides, hands curled forward like talons dangling free. It halted then quickly lowered its head, cocked it to one side, and swung forward.

The small girl gasped as the Raven's face, only inches from hers, hissed and spat. Its eyes focused solely on her.

All at once, Mason stood up out of the rubble, looking dazed, shaking the dust off himself, and trying to figure out what he had clutched in one of his hands. At the sound of items skittering off the concrete floor, the zombie shrieked and spun around, sprinting toward Mason. Shocked by its sudden action, Mason stepped back, swung his hip forward, and let his arm follow. Bone splintered, and gray bits of flesh tore as the hockey mask connected with the undead's large nose and smashed its shards back into its face and brain. Leaping to one side, Mason let the body come to rest on the rubble, then lifted up the front of the mask to reveal what looked like a happy face smeared in blood across it.

Shouts and the cocking of rifles and shotguns pierced the silence of the moment as guards surrounded them and all took aim at Mason. Sprinting between the muzzles and the child, Aaron raised a hand and shouted, "Enough!"

The men hesitated a moment and finally lowered their barrels.

Aaron added, out of breath, "They saved my life... Let them go."

Ethan was already rushing past the men in a hurried walk, dragging the girl, a terrified load in his arms, toward the front doors. Mason looked around wide-eyed and tried to take in the gravity of the situation before rushing behind Ethan.

Standing by the front door as they edged near it and pointing a shotgun at them was Dan. "We're just going to let them go?" yelled Dan. "Just like that?"

Aaron limped out from around the corner, loping toward the front door. "Yes." Then with added force, "They saved my life."

Dan coughed nervously and asked, "What if they tell someone? Our operation—"

Aaron limped up and finally backhanded Dan off his feet, knocking the shotgun away before turning back toward the other men. "Open the doors and let them go."

Men rushed forward, unlatching and unlocking the giant doors. Metal heaved and grated as the doors shifted back and opened up, letting the first rays of the sunrise spill into the warehouse. Mason followed the others and set foot out of the warehouse and into the new day.

13.

Somewhere on the Outskirts of the Shytown Trail

Zombie Civil Rights Group

Present Day

"WHEN THIS BABY HITS eighty-eight miles per hour..." Mason drew a breath. "You're going to see some serious shit."

Mason reached up and slowly pulled down his mask, revealing a teal lightning bolt with a blue outline. He leaned back and braced himself, then began counting, "Eighty-four." The wheels clanged across the broken cement. "Eighty-five." Mason reached down and grabbed handfuls of yarn that all had one end secured to the metal rungs on the side of the cart. "Eighty-six."

Both Donathan and Ashley went into fits of laughter. "Eighty-seven. Oh god, I forgot the time circuits!" Mason exclaimed, then dropped the yarn to reach into the back of the cart and produced an old wooden cuckoo clock with a drill protruding from the back. He squeezed the trigger, the clock's internal gears whirred, and the hands on the face of the clock spun at high speed for a moment. "Time circuits are going, and the flux capacitor is..." Mason paused to look over the side of the cart at the three-pronged symbol he had woven into the mesh with yellow and green yarn before adding, "Capaciting!"

After the cart had gone another ten feet and Donathan and Ashley's laughter began to give way to panting from running and shoving the cart along, Mason finally reached back down, grabbed the handfuls of yarn, and threw them over the side of the cart as he shouted, "Eighty-eight miles per hour!"

Donathan and Ashley gave one final shove and trotted to a halt, appreciating the sight before them. Mason was sitting in the basket of a shopping cart, mask pulled down, patterns of yarn woven into the side of it, and even more yarn hanging off and trailing behind him as it rolled down the slope of the abandoned superhighway.

Donathan's laughter faded, but his grin was wider than ever as Ashley declared, "He looks so serious. I almost believe this will work!" Mason had brought his hands up, mimicking a steering wheel. The cart drifted downhill and picked up speed.

As the wheels rotated across the concrete, the front end of the cart wobbled a bit. The sound of metal scraping concrete suddenly rang out as one of the front wheels was wedged into a crevice, causing the back end of the cart to fly up and catapult Mason forward. As the cart tumbled and smashed end over end, the sounds were deafening. When it finally came to rest, Mason was lying face down on the asphalt, his arms and legs left resting where they had smashed down.

Ashley and Donathan ran up and spun him over, frantically trying to shake him awake. His head hung limply as they shook his shoulders and let go an endless stream of reassurances and begging that he was going to be okay.

After a minute, his eyes jolted open, staring far off as if trying to ascertain something. Donathan and Ashley became quiet in a moment of confusion. Finally, Mason asked in a whisper, "What is that noise?"

Ashley and Donathan had already stood up and been listening to it, the sound of a beat pulsing. The heavy bass of dance music seemed to be carried on the wind across the horizon. Ashley sprinted to the side of the superhighway and peered over. "There's a concert or carnival, or weren't they called raves? Honestly, I don't know what I'm looking at here," she said.

They hurried to help Mason back up, then picked their path across the broken and shattered road and eventually climbed down off the back of the elevated highway, following it on one side past the pillars holding it up. When they finally made it around, they paused a second to take in the scene that was before them.

They had heard the engines of the large construction cranes working long before they had actually seen them. Three large poles had been raised in the center of everything, extending into the sky above, and wires were being draped and dragged from the poles to the edges of the clearing surrounding everything. Small canvas tents had been set in various places under the wired area. Vehicles of all types seemed to be funneling in, following a straight path and circling the compound before parking in various places at the edge of the wire. Throngs of people were walking alongside many of the vehicles but stopping in front of a large main gate that had steel bars, every other bar wrapped in red velvet. A large old broken flatbed of a train car was sitting out front of the scene, where it had permanently come to rest years before. Other hesitant onlookers had gathered near it. Mason, Donathan, and Ashley fell in with them as a man and woman dressed in matching top hats and outfits with red bow ties and gray vests climbed up onto the flatbed. The costumes resembled a cross between formal and party outfits of some kind. The woman was wearing a long skirt made of various fabrics draped below but colored in predominantly red and black. She was short and had full, rosy cherub cheeks and long hair that draped down over her shoulders. Under his top hat, the man had dark hair, trimmed and shining from some unknown product. He had warm eyes, slightly tan skin, and sharp features that seemed to match his tall, lanky body. Small black headsets with mouthpieces hung off both their heads, just under their top hats. The caravan of vehicles drove past behind the scene as the man and woman finished climbing up onto the flatbed. They moved with a sense of grace and showmanship that seemed to pull more of the curious onlookers forward. Finally, they both produced gray microphones from their pockets, and the man leaned into his as he spoke.

"Hey, Ginn?" the man asked.

"Ya, Paul?" the woman replied.

"It seems as though we have a crowd, curious as to what THE event is." A large smile crept across his lips as he spoke.

Ginn drew a deep breath and then strolled across the makeshift stage as vehicles puttered along behind it. In a concerned voice, she replied, "Paul, that's not good. That means they haven't heard of the Knight's Moon Festival."

Paul strolled the other way, matching her path in the opposite direction. His voice feigned pity as he said, "It is a sad... sad day when we find there have been people living their lives, not knowing what Knight's Moon Festival is." He paused to look down at a man in his 40s, with a torn blue t-shirt and faded jeans, who had strolled up to the front of the stage when the announcing began. "So go ahead." Paul motioned to the man. "Ask me what the Knight's Moon Festival is."

Paul crouched down on the edge of the stage and lowered his mic to the man who looked down his nose at it, then in a shocked moment raised his eyes toward Paul and stuttered, "Wh-whas a Knight's M-moon—"

Cutting him off, Paul yanked back the mic, stood up, spun around 360 degrees in one motion, spread his legs wide, flailed one of his arms out, and smiled deeply to the crowd while flashing a showman's eyes and announcing in a grand voice, "THIS... is the moment your life has been building to."

A few cheers rang up from the crowd that had originated from the line of people walking alongside the vehicles behind the stage. Enthusiasm crept in, and Mason pushed forward a ways into the crowd, trying to get a better view.

On stage, Ginn had begun smiling, her red cheeks full of excitement as she chimed in, "What my colleague"— she nodded in Paul's direction—"is trying to say is we are a thirty-six-hour music festival which will lock you in, and for one moment in this godforsaken world, both the undead and the hard life we live shall cease to exist." Her smile had become quite determined by the time the last syllable left her lips.

"Actually, I think there's a bit more to it," Paul added. Ginn just rolled her eyes and strolled past him on stage in a theatrical huff. "You see..." Paul whispered into the mic, "We are an experience."

Paul sighed, then strode off to the left side of the stage and motioned to the caravan. "All of these people in some form or another have got it. Their lives are dedicated to art."

An excited squeal echoed through the quiet and captivated crowd. Mason tried to push his way to the front, but the crowd had become dense, and people were reluctant to give up their spots.

Paul sniffed the air a minute as if approving the moment before he continued, "That's right. They live for the show. They are part our company, our family, only to meet up and caravan in every so often, hopefully to bring little moments of sanity to an otherwise burning world."

"Oh we're dramatic today, are we?" Ginn asked, standing beside Paul, wearing a stern look. "I didn't realize we were going that route." Her sarcastic tone stretched further as she added, "Our Master of Ceremonies is telling you we have four shows—"

Paul interrupted, "Experiences."

"Experiences"—Ginn rolled her eyes once again—"a year. Our following is made up of performers, artists, musicians, fashion designers, brewmasters—"

An excited "What?" echoed up from the audience as Donathan tried to push through toward Mason's position, which was off to the far left side of the stage.

"Dancers, fortune tellers, puppeteers—"

"We seem to be getting a little too detailed," Paul reminded her.

"And loudmouthed emcees." She sneered in Paul's direction. He responded with an unamused glance, and they both seemed to freeze for a moment as laughter rang in front of them.

The hoots and cheers from the crowd were followed by a loud roar of applause.

When the cheers died down, Paul made sure to raise the microphone back to his lips before clearing his throat. He tugged his top hat more securely onto his head and looked back toward the crowd.

"How is this possible, you ask?" Paul motioned toward the cranes and poles behind him. "If you look carefully, you'll see wire being draped from high above the center of the compound over this... what's the name of this abandoned 'fail-ville' behind us, Ginn?"

"Uhh... Clovis?" Ginn seemed to be asking more than stating.

"Really?" Paul replied curiously, pulling the mic away from his mouth and turning toward the desolate city behind them so his words fell off into an echo. "That was Clovis, California? I thought they had a working settlement." Then, drawn back into the moment, he turned to the crowd and said, "What I mean is, those wires being draped over the compound are the highest of technology, a true old-world creation, that when electrified tonight will not only keep out the undead..." He paused and drew a breath before concluding, "But also give one spectacular light show that is easily worth the price of admission!"

The crowd cheered again, and a small Winnebago stopped next to the stage. Women wearing feathered headdresses, masks, and bikinis, each a different color, quickly rushed out of its door and climbed and vaulted up to get onto the train car flatbed stage. Men wearing skin-tight multicolored shorts climbed up from behind the stage. In only a few seconds, the two groups all took up positions around Ginn and Paul and faced the crowd motionlessly, heads cocked slightly toward the emcees and wearing bright smiles. They looked as though they were trying to listen to the conversation the showmen were having. The bass-filled music that had seemed to be drowned out by the two performers was turned up enough that everyone felt the infectious vibe.

The stage had become crowded, and gasps of both excitement and laughter rang up all around Ashley as she tried to push up through the crowd and toward her friends.

Taking a cue, Ginn added, "Prices are near the front gate, the only highly secured entrance and exit into the compound. So for just a little coin—"

"Just a few coins," Paul added in a concerned tone toward the onlookers.

The feathered dancers wearing bright colors wove in and around the emcees as their banter continued.

Ginn's voice boomed as she strode to the other side of the stage, away from Paul. "You will lose yourself in wild laughter, song, dance, alcohol, and maybe the occasional momentary lapse of reason as you fall in love with our show, and dare I say it?"

"Oh, Dare! Dare!..." Paul added as the male dancers swarmed around him, hiding him from sight, and the female dancers took up various positions, some crouching and some kneeling but all looking in various directions from the center of the stage.

The music grew quiet, the dancers froze, and Ginn looked out at the audience and said in a serious tone, "For thirty-six hours—"

Out of sight, Paul still interrupted, "Just thirty-six fun-filled hours—"

"Life will seem carefree." She grinned and looked up at the sky as the last word fell from her lips.

The crowd of male dancers on stage shifted about, finally revealing Paul, grinning devilishly and sitting on a throne made from the men's kneeling legs and full torsos. He leaned back, putting his left arm around the nearest man's neck and pulling him in close. Then he turned to face the crowd's laughter and excitement.

Ginn chuckled at Paul, then very quickly turned to the crowd and said in a serious tone, "Of course, there is the matter of the blood test at the front gate."

Paul added in a fatherly manner, "We have to make sure none of us is going to become a zombie in the middle of our show. But it's for safety, and just one tiny prick—"

"One tiny prick, Paul?" Ginn asked suddenly.

Paul looked over one of his shoulders to the man kneeling on his left and then over his right shoulder, then turned back to the audience and said in an amused tone, "Well…"

After more laughter subsided, he slowly raised the microphone back up and said calmly, "Look… You're going to go your whole lives…" He drew breath and, spreading his arms to stretch and look comfortable from where he was sitting, added, "and you're never going to live this moment over."

Paul sprang to his feet as Ginn raised her hands cheering, and all the dancers scattered around them to begin sliding and shifting in a well-rehearsed number with the music cascading around them.

The audience members danced and laughed as well. Bodies shifted around Mason until one firmly took hold of his shoulder and spun him around until he was staring at the barrel of a snub-nosed .38 only inches from his face.

A grim-looking man with a dark, dirty sweater stood behind the pistol and stared back at Mason with a look of hate and desperation. "Don't you fucking flinch. Give me your money and that gun."

Mason looked dumbfounded as he stared cross-eyed at the dark, tinted gunmetal, his machine gun still hanging off his side.

The man shoved the pistol forward a few inches and added in a darker tone, "Do you think I'm fucking joking? Give me your gun and your money, or I'll put a bullet between your eyes right n—"

"What?" a shout rang out directly behind him as Mason stumbled and fell backward. The full force of Ashley sprinting and leaping propelled her entire body over Mason as her foot smashed into the man's face in one quick motion. The crowd suddenly shoving around her had sent both of them plummeting forward and into the other audience members.

Ashley raised her head from the ground, propped up on her arms, and looked through the sand and dust across the small clearing. Other audience members scrambled to back away from her and the man. He was already reaching toward the pistol only a few feet from him. Ashley, still separated by several feet, reached down for the rifle slung on her side, only to find it had been lost in the chaos of the moment. In one motion, she reached up and behind her, unsheathed her bat, and flung it over her shoulder, spinning it end over end into the man's hand. Screaming in pain, the man clutched his hand to his sweater-covered chest and, after one split second of rage, adopted a determined look and lunged across for the pistol with his other hand.

Donathan felt the beat and surged forward. For a moment, the whole scene around him moved slowly. He gasped, realizing this was new. The performers on stage looked frozen and dumbstruck by the scene below them. Only Paul had a look of rage and was motioning to some large individuals offstage with one hand, his other hand holding the microphone in their direction, its arc moving very slowly toward the scene. Dust hung in the air. Mason, his jaw open, was sitting in the sand, his machine gun lying on its side next to him, still slung over his shoulder. Audience members seemed to be moving at a snail's pace as their legs and arms were flexed in panicked positions trying to flee the scene. Ashley was staring across the clearing with a look of frustration and rage on her tiny face. The would-be thief's hand was curled into his chest, and a murderous look hung in his eyes as his other hand was reaching across and had nearly grabbed the gun.

Donathan ran up between them and then turned to look at Ashley, her face still fuming with anger, then back at the man and then back at Ashley before he reached down, picked up the pistol, and ran to Ashley, tucking it into the palm of her hand.

In a moment the scene pulsed back into motion.

Everyone gasped and grew silent as they realized something had rushed through and changed the outcome of the moment. Only Paul seemed to not have noticed it and was screaming obscenities and commands until a window finally opened on a large RV that stopped in the column of vehicles behind the stage. Ginn quickly ran to the back of the stage and stuck her head in the window as Paul quieted down. After a few seconds, she backed out of the dark window, holding something small in her left hand, and ran across the stage.

"Just him. Just the sweater guy." She motioned in his direction while leaping off the flatbed stage. Large men rushed forward toward the thief. Ginn ran up to a very shocked Ashley and placed a card in her hand, then, somewhat out of breath, said, "Waterfalz wishes to extend her apologies for the unsavory element who appeared and wants to invite your friends to speak with her later tonight. She also waives the price of entrance for you and your friends." Ginn finally croaked out the last syllable and drew a gasping breath while leaning forward to place a hand on one of her knees.

As the sweater-clad man was dragged, shouting, away from the crowd, Paul chimed back in and soothed people's nerves with quick-witted comments about how he wanted people to behave "hyphy and not knifey."

Donathan and Mason helped Ashley to her feet, and they all gathered around and stared at the card in the palm of her hand, which read in tiny black print, The Great Mystic Waterfalz: One free reading.

14.

Knight's Moon Festival

Zombie Civil Rights Group

Present Day

THE LINE STRETCHED for about an hour after the stage show concluded, and the onlookers pushed toward the front gate. Everyone from that crowd seemed to be enthusiastically asking Ashley, Donathan, and Mason how they knew these people or what had happened during the performance. Donathan had used it as a cue to ask if anyone knew Princess Jae. One person had mentioned that he had heard her name once or twice in the northern parts of the state, but he couldn't remember exactly where since he had been following the Festival for the last three years.

The closer they pushed toward the door, the more they noticed that most people here had been following the Festival and were trying to find some way to get employed directly by them. It was a moving enclave of performers, and aside from the occasional murmurs amongst the participants, very few people seemed to know any more details on where The Knight's Moon Festival came from or who controlled it.

The crowd broke near the front of the line to reveal makeshift booths of curtains and rods. Every so often, a person would walk out from behind the line of booths toward the front gate. Some would pause to open bags and backpacks and begin drawing out brightly colored clothing or various other accessories that seemed very out of place for the Shytown Trail. After a moment, a booth's curtain would slide open as a festival employee shouted out "Next!" It wasn't until they approached the front of the line that they could see most of the employees were wearing brightly colored clothing and various beaded bracelets, and a few of them had colored hair.

Hearing the word "Next!" Mason took the opportunity to slide between and around two people pressing forward and beat their pace into the booth. As he stepped into the room and the curtain slid behind him, he realized he was standing in a mock-up of an old doctor's office. A teal-covered gurney stood in the center of the room, and next to it was a syringe without a needle, a box of plastic gloves, and a large cardboard box on the ground next to it labeled Tests in bright, colorful graffiti-style letters. Across the room were two small cabinets with rollaway wheels on them, and perched on top of one cabinet was a glass jar of tongue depressors, each one with a different clown made of pipe-cleaners and puffy paint. A poster was hung near the back of the booth, showing a doctor in clown makeup, holding a balloon with permanent ink marker writing above it labeled Exit and followed by an arrow pointing past the clown-doctor toward a slit in the back curtains. The thought occurred to Mason that he could stay all day here, just studying the contents of the room.

A young woman wearing furry white leg warmers over tall boots with matching white shorts and a tank top walked up from one of the front corners of the room. Her face was painted white with long black hash marks over each eye to mimic a porcelain doll, but she wore a light green surgical mask over the bottom half of her face.

The man who had closed the curtains walked up past Mason toward the gurney with the bedside table. He was wearing an old black sports jersey with orange letters that read SF GIANTS across the front. Dark blue flared jeans covered his legs, and several beaded bracelets snaked up his left arm. His hair was red and his skin pale. The man paused at the table and began pulling on a new pair of rubber gloves he had dragged out of the box with a quick flick of his right arm. A loud thwack sounded as he stretched the last glove over his hand. He faced Mason and announced, "Please take off your shirt."

Mason stepped forward toward the gurney, looked from the woman to the man in a moment of confusion, set down his machine gun, and pulled off his kevlar vest and set it on the ground. Everything felt light, and the air on his sweat-soaked, shirt-covered back felt cool. Mason hadn't realized how uncomfortable he was in that thing until just then.

The woman grew impatient and stepped forward, tugging his shirt up and asking in a curt tone, "First festival?"

Mason mumbled, "Yes," and then pulled the shirt from her hands and up over his shoulders and head.

Once the shirt was off, the man motioned him forward, adding, "It's wonderful, you'll love it, it'll change your life, I need your arm," all in one breath.

Mason shuffled forward and then paused in front of the gurney before the man nodded for him to sit, reaching down into the cardboard box next to him.

The man hurriedly said, "Okay, we're going to need to draw a little bit of blood, I need you to look toward the clown at the end of the room, and you're going to feel a sharp sting from the needle, keep looking at the clown." Mason's eyes focused on the clown, but a moment of doubt filled him. "Drawing blood for a festival?" he thought. His head slowly turned toward the man's work. The man was staring intently at Mason's arm and jammed a needle three times into Mason's upper arm, just under his shoulder.

Mason yelped, and the man looked up and locked gazes with him before dropping the needle back into the far side of the cardboard box. Mason started to question why there was no syringe attached when the woman yanked him around by the shoulder and handed him a small red ticket and his shirt.

"Vehicle Alpha-34," she said.

"What?" Mason asked nervously.

"Your weapons and armor." She paused to sigh, and her surgical mask flexed for a moment. Then she continued in a very monotone voice, "They will be in vehicle Alpha-34. Should something happen, we'll go to rally point red, like the ticket."

"Wait, I can't—" Mason felt two sets of hands on his chest as his balance was tipped backward and he was forcefully shoved out the back of the booth by both the man and the woman.

As he stood staring at the back of the curtain for a moment, he heard them both simultaneously shout, "Next!" Suddenly he was very conscious of how loud the music was here. He thought about rushing back inside to grab his weapons, then decided to wait at the front gate for Donathan, knowing he'd have a plan.

As Mason reached the front gate he noticed vehicles still filtering in on the far side of the gate. A small woman, with a purple ribbon braided through her hair and a green-and-white checkered jumper like those old-fashioned clowns used to wear, motioned him forward. After a moment of shouting over the music, he realized she was asking to see his ticket. He showed it to her, and she again repeated his items were going to be in "Alpha-34." Shrugging, he stepped through the giant gate of iron and red-velvet strips, then stopped mid-step to stare at the view before him.

A crowd pulsed to life on all sides as people laughed, danced, and sprinted in various directions before him. Brightly colored outfits and baggy pants seemed to appear on all sides. Hands palmed glowsticks, water bottles, beer mugs, and candied apples. Many people wore backpacks made of stuffed animals, paint on their faces, or ribbons in their hair. Brightly colored paintings were spread across most things in sight, including the white canvas tents, which were vending items or handing out water. The tents were spread around the sides of the compound, and many were almost blocked from sight by the sheer number of people crossing paths. The throng of vehicles snaked a winding trail away from the front gate. They organized, parking in neat rows on the far side of the compound. To Mason's left was a large stage, with pulsing multicolored lights draping every inch of it, spots twisting and spectrums shifting to match the beat of the electronic dance music. Oversized speakers were lined up around the side and rear of the stage. Three large metal poles were perched strategically in the center of the compound with wire cables extending in all directions from their apexes, creating a large fence around the assemblage of people. Just under their tops were small crow's nests that had a few people wearing the same carnival jumpers of differing colors dancing on top of them. Small people, dwarfed by the distance between Mason and them, could be seen climbing a rickety set of stairs on top of the arm of the construction crane, which was parked off-center near the massive wire ceiling supports. The arm extended up toward the crow's nests. The whole mass of people seemed to bob and weave to the beat as they went about their adventures. The sun had dipped below the horizon, and the sky was lit up with crimson hues that blended into indigo farther into the heavens.

"They took my weapon," Ashley said as she stepped up next to Mason, facing the same direction toward the crowd. Her voice didn't seem to have much care in it. Her eyes were wide and full of wonder, and her breath seemed stifled a bit by the sheer amazement of the scene before them.

"At least they didn't take your bat," Donathan added, stepping up on her far side, "and I've still got my Bowie knife, so there's that." Donathan turned to his right quite suddenly and said, "And then there's that."

Mason cocked his head in that direction, studied the sign in front of the canvas tent and then asked, "Why would they sell ghosts?"

Ashley's gaze slid to her right and then back toward the crowd, "You mean spirits, right? Not that kind of spirits."

The crowd parted, and Frankie and Eddie came sprinting out from the center of the crowd toward the gate. Eddie had a rainbow wig on, and Frankie had his shirt off. Both were grinning from ear to ear.

Ashley's gaze drifted off the crowd and locked onto Eddie and Frankie, who both froze in place and donned matching looks of shock. After a moment, Ashley snapped forward half a step and spread her arms out in one quick motion as though she were about to sprint at them. As they turned tail and ran back into the dense crowd, Mason, Donathan, and Ashley all chuckled together and then turned their attention back to the festival.

Everyone tensed up for a second as an electronically amplified snap rang out across the speakers, followed by the pulse of a low hum. A second later, the bottom of the pyramid, a mass of wires, lit up, glowing a neon blue. The light surrounded the entire compound, and small tendrils of cyan light popped and hissed as they extended from one coil to another. The hum added a little more bass as it extended farther up the wires, slowly creeping toward the apex as if it were a sluggish puddle of water spilled on a granite countertop.

As Donathan admired the light show, he said in a matter of fact tone, "Strange technology."

The final coils lit, and the whole compound glowed blue. Colors from the tents seemed even more vibrant and bright, the crowd's makeup and jewelry glowed, and even the sunset's blending of different shades seemed amplified by the fallout of electrical light. The bass-fueled dance music's volume grew a bit louder, and the gentle hum of the circuit around them faded into it.

Ashley finally stopped looking so entranced and turned to Donathan, asking, "What do we do about our weapons?"

Donathan asked, "What ticket did they give you?"

"Charlie-10," she replied.

"I have Alpha-34," Mason added.

"I have Alpha-34 too," Donathan shrugged. "What can we do?" His body was already edging back toward the tent labeled Spirits. "I guess just have a good time and meet up back at this spot in a few hours."

"Wait!" Mason shouted excitedly. "I have a project."

"This one will be good, I bet." Ashley's voice seemed to have the same excitement as his.

Mason and Donathan stopped for a second and looked quizzically at Ashley. One of Mason's eyebrows was arched at a strange angle, giving him the look of both shock and confusion as they all stood staring at one another.

"What? I can't get enthusiastic just once?" Ashley asked in a huff.

Mason slowly lowered his eyebrow, then took two steps toward the crowd, still looking at Ashley with apprehension before finally snapping his head forward and flagging down a young woman wearing baggy pants and a t-shirt holding two red glowsticks. "Can I have those?" She stopped, nodded, and handed him the glowsticks but continued to stand in place. He did the same thing to two other passersby until he was holding one yellow, one orange, two red, and two green glowsticks in a stack in his left fist. He went to walk back to Donathan and Ashley, then realized all of the people he had taken them from were still standing and staring at him.

"No, I meant have." Looking curious for a moment, they still stood there, so Mason waved his right arm in a frustrated motion and shouted over the music, "Go away get out of here I need this for art!" Each person's face looked puzzled as they turned and walked away, blending back into the group of people.

Mason handed a separate pair of glowsticks to both Ashley and Donathan then said in an excited shout, while motioning in various directions, "Light art! I'm going to go to that side of the compound; Ashley, you go over there—"

Ashley asked, "I thought I saw an old-timey Ferris wheel near the far side of the stage. Can I—"

Mason interrupted her but kept the same elation in his voice, "Yes, fine. Ashley goes there, I go there, and Donathan, you stay here. Look up and in five minutes time, when you see the signal, you do the same."

Without questioning it, Ashley rushed forward into the crowd toward the stage. Mason reached up and pulled on his mask for a second to make sure it was still sitting raised on his head before he slipped off in the other direction, and Donathan stood in place, looking from the sky to the canvas tent housing the alcohol and back. Each person that stepped past him into the tent received a frustrated glance from him.

Donathan had been tugging at one of the seams on his duster when five minutes passed. The music had begun to crescendo as bass beats rose into a fast, rhythmic twang and an electronic kick snare. A flash went up on his far left side as a glowstick went sailing into the air on that side of the compound. A second one soared up from the direction of the stage. Donathan pulled one arm back and threw his first, then his second glowstick.

Lights shot up all around and in front of Donathan as the rest of the crowd followed suit. Each time one of the sticks fell out of the sky and disappeared, it was replaced by someone throwing one back up into the sky. Obviously, people were fishing them off the ground and throwing them back up. The crowd cheered. As the light from the glowsticks trailed through the sky, the arcs of the thrown sticks all rose up and then fell back away, leaving a path of colors as they did. It looked like a moving, living dome of light under the already blue electrically charged coils above it.

Donathan grinned wider than ever as he said under his breath, "That kid is a master artist..." His smile faded as he added, "Cursed to live in this world."

Drawing a breath, he glanced back up at the tent and finally said to himself, "Well, at least there's tonight." Then he stepped into the tent.

An hour later, Paul and Ginn were back on stage, breathing more energy into the crowd over the electronic music. The stage behind them was covered in digital screens all broadcasting their images from various angles as they spoke into the microphones carrying their voices out into the party-filled night.

"...and that's technically how it's done." Paul was finishing up an anecdote. The crowd responded with laughter. Each screen flashed to his face for a moment as the lights behind them flashed green and disco whistles echoed rhythmically through a House song.

Paul turned toward Ginn, who was standing on the far left side of the stage. "I need a victim—I mean...a fresh face for an interview."

Ginn leaned over, hanging off the stage, and fished to pull a random person out from the cramped crowd below. Finally she dragged a sweaty, glassy-eyed girl with long straight brunette hair up onto the edge of the stage. She had several plastic beaded necklaces and was wearing an extremely short pink skirt and a t-shirt that had a cartoon bear on it. Ginn held the microphone up under her mouth.

All at once the girl gushed out, "OHMYGOD I've been wanting to get up here FOREVER—" The video screens behind the stage showed a horrified look on Paul's face as the girl continued to swoon. "I-AM-SO-EXCITED my life is spent following the festival and TRYING to get hired—" The video monitors on stage showed Ginn's face with a disappointed and concerned look on it, and the girl still didn't stop to breathe. "I-LOVE-YOU-GUYS-SO-MUCH I have followed the show for at least two years and—"

Paul interrupted, "Ginn, throw it back."

In one quick motion, Ginn shoved the girl back off the stage and into the crowd, then fished through the crowd again. After a moment, she dragged a young man wearing a sweaty t-shirt, brown slacks, and striped sneakers onto the stage. His right hand was holding a raised hockey mask securely onto his head as he stepped out of the crowd. His eyes were bright and full of life.

"Interesting... This shows promise," Paul remarked as Ginn nodded back with the pride of a job well done as she slid the microphone under Mason's chin.

Mason hesitated and then added, "Uhh... hi?"

Paul smirked and asked, "What's your name?"

"It's uhh Mason. Mason Meeks."

"Mason Meeks, are you enjoying the party?" Paul asked quizzically.

"Oh, it's amazing. I've never seen anything like it."

The screens behind the stage lit up as the green colors shifted to yellow light. Paul, Ginn, and Mason were all showed on different screens observing the entire interview. The music wavered for a moment, and the volume came down a bit.

Paul looked amused. "So what do you do in the space between laughter?"

Mason smiled, squared his shoulders, and stood up a bit taller, "I'm an artist. I make art."

The screens behind them all showed Ginn rolling her eyes as she slowly pulled the microphone back.

Paul sighed openly into the mic and added in a monotone voice, "Oh good, another artist looking for work. That never happens. I'd sure love to see your work sometime." As the last syllable trailed off, Paul stuck his tongue out and made a frustrated thbbbt sound.

Each screen cut to show Mason and Ginn as Ginn stepped backward and prepared to shove Mason back into the crowd.

Sensing what was about to happen, Mason quickly took a determined step forward, reached up, and lowered his mask to reveal a picture of Paul's and Ginn's faces, side by side, staring up at the stars as a bright red glowstick sailed through the painted sky.

The cameras linked to the various screens on stage all zoomed and focused on his masked face as he raised his arms out and then leaned forward and bowed. The crowd erupted with cheering and applause.

After a moment, it died down as Paul's shocked face appeared on screen. Finally, he re-raised his microphone to his mouth and added, "I stand corrected. You are an artist." Ginn nodded across the stage in Mason's direction.

Someone in the crowd in front of the stage was leaping up and down and shouting "Mason" repeatedly. Mason raised his mask and peered forward to see Ashley beckoning him toward the crowd. Mason sprang forward off the stage and into the crowd.

Ginn's voice echoed off the stage, "And just like that, the artist is gone."

Paul reminded her, "Real artists don't need recognition."

Ginn's laugh was genuine and heavy for a moment before she asked, "Then what are you?"

"I am..." Paul drew a breath, looked out onto the crowd, and continued, "a work of art."

The crowd laughed as the music's volume rose back to its previous level.

Ashley had dragged Mason back to where the crowd thinned near the middle of the complex before she turned back toward him. She was grinning ear to ear before she even spoke. "I saw you on stage! This night has been amazing. Look, someone gave me a sunflower and candy, and I think these people are completely fucking insane, but I've never felt so safe or had so much fun in my life—"

Donathan strolled up out of the crowd, swaying for a moment.

Mason and Ashley both burst out laughing. After a minute, Mason was leaning forward trying to catch his breath. When he looked up, his eyes locked onto something before he turned back to his friends and asked, "That card said Waterfalls with a z, right?" Motioning past himself, Mason pointed toward a violet tent with ribbons and symbols painted in blue all over it. The word *Waterfalz* was written in calligraphy across the front flap of the tent. The top of the tent was painted in a slightly darker shade of violet. Under the blue electric light from the glowing coils above, the tent seemed out of place. The colors made it resemble some unknown precious gem.

"Well, I guess we should go inside," Donathan remarked and stumbled forward.

"Why not?" Ashley asked. Mason followed his friends inside.

15.

Knight's Moon Festival

Zombie Civil Rights Group

Present Day

THE MUSIC'S BEAT seemed muffled and far off as they stepped through the canvas opening and into the room. Smoke, incense, and sage hung thick in the air. Candles flickered, causing shadows to creep and drift about the lilac-colored tarpaulin hanging overhead. In the back of the tent, several dark-jade-colored ferns clung to the wall from baskets fastened to the bar of the tent frame. A dim indigo light was angled up and through the plants' tendrils running down in different approaches to line the rear wall of the shelter, creating fractals of light, shadow, and indigo. A small beige table had been set up in the center of the room with a few tarot cards set in a pattern. Eerie, intricate designs crisscrossed their faces. Next to the cards was a dish with two different-sized candles whose wax had trickled down over their edges as the flames hung on the wicks just above. Behind the table was an old wooden folding chair with various occult symbols etched into its varnished wood. A small shaft of blue-tinted moonlight angled into the room from an opening near the back of the tent. The ringing of wind chimes drifted in from the edge of eternity.

"I'm going to be sick," Donathan announced and spun around swiftly to run out the way he had come in, only to find himself face-to-face with a dark-skinned woman giving him a stern gaze, her wild eyes full of judgment. Her hair cascaded over her shoulders, thick and curled. Her shirt, a light blue satin, shimmered in the dark room. Her dress was swaths of cloth and silks, and around her waist hung a rope belt wrapped several times around with various fresh herbs strung through it and clinging to the outside of her dress. Every finger and thumb of her hands glistened with jewels from various rings.

Donathan swayed for a moment when faced with a stranger just inches from his face, but the second her voice creaked forth, his body seemed to steady, and his motions were suddenly more sober.

"Ay, ju 'af come to me for gui-dence. Tainted. Don' ju be trowin' up on my floor," she said, stepping past the group. As she crossed the room, one of her arms reached out and trailed through the shadows bringing more life from the hidden wind chimes hanging off to the left side of the tent. Their tinkling filled the air. She paused for a moment at her table and let her hands paw across the tarot cards, her head hanging over them as if studying their mystical inscriptions and searching for something far off. "What ees it ju haf come to see da Great andt Mystical Waterfalz about?"

Mason chirped up first, "We have a card. We were given it out front of the—"

"AH, DA HEROES!" Waterfalz interrupted. "Da great champi-yons of da day." At this point, she swung around the table and sat in the chair with the cards in front of her. Her head lowered close to the table, and the shaded indigo light combined with the flicker of candles reflected off the contours of her face and made her eyes look dark and distant. As her shoulders hunched forward, her head twitched a moment, and her arms vanished under the table as she spoke in a strained voice, "I knaw ju betta' dan ju knaw juself. Ju powers...dey are growing—"

"This is a crock of shit." Ashley had finally had enough. "We're just supposed to believe this New Orleans Voodoo Queen?"

"New Orleans?" Waterfalz's accent had suddenly vanished and been replaced with a Midwest twang. "That was Jamaican, and girl, I'm from Ohio," she said curtly. Her body was still lowered over the cards and her face wore a look of determination. Finally, she took hold of one of the candles, stood up, and backed away from the table of cards, lifting a cigarette to her lips. "Found my damn cigarette finally." The tip of the cigarette grew amber and smoldered as she stared cross-eyed down it toward the candle's flame, her lungs inhaling repetitive short breaths as two of her ring-covered fingers clutched the filter between them.

Her right hand looked as if it had a mind of its own as it lowered and eased the candle back to the dish on the table while she shut her eyes and let her entire body puff in a deep drag from the cigarette. Gasping, she let the smoke leave her lungs and rush past her lips toward the ceiling of the tent before she continued in her normal voice.

"The world is alive, you see. It's a living, breathing organism, and she's sick right now. Sick with death or the lack of it, which shows itself after sunset in grinning and gnashing teeth. But never forget that she's alive and that she's always listening." Waterfalz drew another drag from her cigarette and then stared for a moment at her audience to make sure she had their attention. After a moment, she motioned for them to come closer. Mason stepped forward first, Ashley followed a half second after, and Donathan stumbled and stepped into the table, almost knocking it back over before shuddering straight.

Waterfalz's gaze had become judgmental again as she stared down her nose back at Donathan. "I would say it's a weakness but... it wouldn't matter, would it?" Turning her back to the three, Waterfalz picked through the tendrils of the ferns and changed their positioning across the back wall. She continued her story, "Every time the world has needed them, they are born. Some call them heroes. Others will refer to them as champions. Sometimes they're warriors, shamans, or even called saviors. Whether the call is due to a disaster or someone gaining and using powers for unnatural means, the reality is they're just her answer. When things have gotten dark for the denizens of this planet, she listens and calls to the heavens for them to be released. For them to dance and hopefully grow life again from the destruction that follows their wake."

Turning around suddenly, she let both of her arms fall to her sides, the cigarette leaving a small blazing trail as it dropped. The music faded from existence as the smoke eased around her, twisting and twirling its slow path through her curls. The gentle noise from the wind chime evaporated, and the light in the room intensified into a bright purple haze. Her voice echoed into the night as she spoke. "Heroes are always born into a world that needs it. Their mystical qualities are often ignored by history, but they're there just the same."

She paused to raise the cigarette back to her lips and inhale. The tent seemed to flex inward and inhale with her. "Cleopatra, the Egyptian queen, oozed charisma. Most saw it as she was simply gorgeous and the very essence of royalty, everything a follower could want. But the reality is she had a power that could charm whole civilizations to their knees. Her power was so great that only when she was fooled into thinking all was lost, did her power finally fail her, and she took her own life."

Waterfalz's figure slid to one side of the tent in one fluid motion. Her legs had gone through the gentle motion of walking, but the rest of her body coasted along in an ethereal manner. "The Native Americans had a Champion named Crazy Horse who could not be killed by any manner of bullets or ammunition. Eventually, he had to be forced to surrender his own life because his powers were too great. Of course, your talents are nowhere near as developed as them." She glided back to the center of the room and seemed to let her image ground itself before continuing. "Your talents are forces of destruction to those who would oppose you, and in a world built on death and oppression, this may be exactly what we need to shake the cobwebs free, but you should always remember: one society's hero is another society's villain."

Stepping past the table and directly in front of Mason, she reached up and took gentle hold of the headphones hanging around his neck. "I see the three of you have already figured out what the ancient Romans knew about music as they beat war drums to guide their soldiers into battle." She let the headphones drop and stared for a moment into Mason's eyes, which were already filled with wonderment. "Many things have a beat, and using it can lead you to victory; it can rip your defeat from the hands of your enemies, and it can take hold of your soul just when you need it and pull you kicking and screaming"—her voice had dropped to a whisper—"through darkness."

She stepped past Mason toward Ashley, who squared her shoulders and stood a bit taller, then looked shocked as Waterfalz flicked her hand past and continued on, halting in front of Donathan. "You." Her voice had a strange accusation-filled tone to it.

Donathan swayed a moment and tried to mumble something before Waterfalz shushed him, holding up her index finger inches from his face. Then she slowly pointed it forward and lowered it toward his chest. "You are a Champion of Maneuver. That much is true. Your actions can even ripple the very fabric of time." Donathan's eyes grew wide as she continued, "Your power is the most apparent but also the most volatile. It doesn't work like theirs does. While you control it well, for now, if you're not conscious of the situation"—her voice grew dark—"it can't help you. You don't even know what you are."

Her small frame turned and glided in front of Ashley, and then her head swiveled to face her, letting her body follow suit. Waterfalz's dark eyes had taken on a pale hue in the light. "For all your sharp tongue, your skill lies in your body and determination. You are the Champion of Dexterity." Ashley's stern face melted away and was replaced by a stunned look.

"How did you—" Ashley began to ask, only to be interrupted by Waterfalz's sharp voice.

"Your power comes when you need it. Of course, it can be controlled. Your will and your sheer determination to survive, to achieve victory, and to save the lives of those you love bring it from within." Waterfalz's voice changed again, to a bold tone. "When you need it, you'll be able to throw thread through the eye of a needle." Ashley looked confused for a moment before Waterfalz turned and glided away toward Mason.

As she slid directly in front of Mason, he lowered his head and stuttered, "I don't... I don't have any power."

Waterfalz cackled, and the tent's light seemed to flicker and mimic her movement, casting shadows of devilish smiles about the room. When she finally stopped, a slight breeze gusted through the tent. "In World War II, there was a great soldier called Audie Murphy. He sent over a hundred of the enemy to their death. His very presence on the battlefield would change things in his favor. He was awarded the Medal of Honor twice, an award given only to those who made great sacrifices, sometimes including their own lives. He always lived." Her head edged forward until her hollow eyes were staring directly into Mason's. "You are the Champion of Luck. When you hear the beat, it puts you on the path you need to be. Things fall into place around you, sometimes quite literally. You're more in tune with it than the others, and it shows"—the cigarette floated up from below her face and slid into place between her lips—"in your creations."

"What type of heroes are we?" a voice rang out from the door. The smoke fell away suddenly. The light of the room jolted back to normal, and the beat of the music from outside faded back in as the cigarette fell from Waterfalz's lips. She took hold of Mason's shoulders and swung her head to one side around his, staring with big dark eyes toward the canvas opening of the tent.

Standing in front of the opening were Frankie with Eddie. Next to them was a small blonde girl with straight hair that hung just past her shoulders. Pink pants matched her pink knit beanie and contrasted well with her white t-shirt. Round glasses hung snugly on her nose, and for a moment she looked embarrassed. Her tiny body seemed to shy away from the two men standing next to her as she let her gaze come to rest on the ground just in front of her feet.

Frankie said, "I mean us," then motioned between him and Eddie. "Us two, here."

Waterfalz did not look amused. "Unlikely heroes," she said and then motioned Ashley, Donathan, and Mason toward the back exit of the tent. Strutting past the three as they made their way out the back, her voice chimed in a warm tone, "Sorry, little one, I didn't see you there."

The cold air struck them all with force as Ashley led them out of the tent and back into the night.

16.

Knight's Moon Festival

Zombie Civil Rights Group

Present Day

THE BEAT HAD CHANGED. The crowd seemed restless, and people were no longer dancing but instead looking nervously toward the stage. Masses of people trotted about and scanned the mob with panicked eyes. From their vantage point, the members of the ZCR could see most of the crowd scurry frantically before them toward the stage area. Donathan stopped in front of Waterfalz's tent near an old wooden picnic table and motioned for everyone to wait as they tried to figure out what was different about the festival.

As if answering their curiosity, the volume of the music lowered, and Paul chimed in across the loudspeaker in a dry tone. "The Knight's Moon Festival and all of her lovely patrons would like to thank members of the Protectorate Army for making an appearance here this evening." The lighting behind the screens on stage was dark blue, and each one framed an image of Paul with a very unamused look. After a moment, the cameras flashed images of various armor-clad soldiers wearing their distinctive masks and standing near wild-eyed partygoers who were giving them wary looks and a foot or two of space.

Ginn picked up the cue as Paul paced to the back of the stage. "We can only assume they are here for security purposes and—"

Paul walked back toward the front of the stage with a confident stride and something in his left hand. He placed one foot forward as all the lighting on stage turned dark red. His voice boomed out of the microphone as he shouted, "EVERYONE just SHUT THE FUCK UP!" and his left hand swung up before him, brandishing a MAC-10 fully automatic firearm.

The music screeched off violently. A collective gasp was heard, and for a moment the crowd froze. The only thing that seemed to be moving was the look of confusion that charged across the faces of everyone in the audience. The night's chill held complete silence with the exception of a few loud crickets singing from outside the compound. About thirty seconds passed until, all at once, Paul chirped in with, "I'm just kidding—it's plastic," as he held it out and tapped the barrel against the microphone's base.

The crowd issued forth laughter and applause. The screens showed Paul smiling widely with a mischievous grin on his face as Ginn stepped forward at his side. He brought the mic up slowly to his lips and then in the middle of chuckling, dropped his tone and said with a serious voice, "But theirs aren't fake."

The screens behind the stage flashed up several different shots. Each image featured people edging away from what the camera was centered on, usually a sneering person in face paint and a brightly colored clown jumper holding a rifle or pistol at each soldier's helmeted head. Some of the members of the Knight's Moon were wearing wigs, and as the screens flashed through different scenes, each angle showed someone holding a different type of weapon. One person even held a colonial musket to a soldier's head.

Paul's voice echoed through the crowd's fearful banter. "Now here's what's going to happ—"

The camera cut to Ginn's face as her breath drew in nervously and she donned a frightened look. Her tone was reserved as she said, "Oh, Paul." Her voice gained an accusatory sound as she turned around, giving her back to the audience and finishing with, "She's here."

The crowd had begun to part near the middle of the compound, and cameras on stage seemed to be searching for the source. Finally, one came to rest on a woman strolling through people as they sprinted past. She was wearing the same armor the other soldiers wore except it was white with blue edging. All the cameras focused on her, and several were zooming in for closeups as she stepped up to where the large construction crane had parked earlier. She placed a tiny hand upon its steel casing near one of the doors just above its tires. The sound of buckling metal shrieked through the night as the top arm of the crane ripped backward on itself, followed by the steel near its base shuddering and then collapsing, toppling its mass forward. The crowd scurried to escape its falling figure, but screams rang out from those not quick enough to sprint away.

Donathan announced, "It's time to leave," then both he and Ashley spun around on their heels to run, only to find Mason facing them, standing on the picnic table.

Mason's whole demeanor seemed more interested than fearful. Ashley and Donathan exchanged confused glances before Mason pointed across the sprinting, fear-filled people toward the blue-and-white-armored woman's image on the screen and announced to his friends, "She has a beat."

The screen suddenly shifted to an enraged and serious-looking version of Ginn, who spoke through pursed lips pulled back and showing a small amount of her teeth. "Barbie... fetch Beauty."

The screens all cut to an image of a woman standing above the crowd on one of the platforms attached to the long poles towering overhead. She wore the porcelain doll makeup. She was wearing white furry leg warmers over tall boots with matching white shorts and a tank top. Mason recognized her from his earlier encounter in the makeshift hospital room. She nodded, then climbed over the guardrail on the platform. Facing the platform, she white-knuckle-gripped the rail before arching her back, then leaped up and backward away from it. For a moment, her body almost skimmed the electricity surging through the wires over the compound, her hair feathering out in a disheveled manner around her before gravity took hold and she fell toward the earth. A few screens on the stage focused on a large undecorated tent near the rear of the compound. The tent's canvas shifted and shuffled forward, tearing tent stakes and cords from the ground. A second later, it leaped up to meet her halfway.

Screams issued forth as both canvas and girl fell to the ground in a huddled mass. Shots rang out in the night. The crowd became frantic and sprinted in random directions around the compound. The screens showed several soldiers with rifles at the ready, edging up to surround the pile of canvas. One in particular stepped through the dust and darkness and poked at the canvas with his rifle's barrel before turning to shrug at one of his comrades.

The canvas came to life, and a large heap with long legs snapped free of it, then smashed the soldier, sending him screaming through the air. Slowly, the canvas peeled away as it stood up and stretched. White legs gave way to a bulbous pink-and-gray-speckled body with a human's torso and legs dangling in front of it like a marionette. The drooping body wore a torn old blue t-shirt and ripped jean shorts. Perched on the top of the creature, seated comfortably on its round bulb of weight behind the legs, was the small woman with an evil grin. The creature held the body aloft and let its bulk rear back as it issued forth an unearthly roar. Its dangling body's hijacked limbs trembled as the mouth stretched unnaturally. The sound ripped through the crowd. The small woman on the creature's carapace swung her head back and matched the monstrosity's scream.

"What the *FUCK* is THAT?" Ashley shouted over the roaring.

"It's a Shat," Mason answered. "I never knew they came in colors."

Donathan commented, "The name certainly fits."

"I think it's on our side, though," Mason added.

The Shat and its rider were still roaring. Finally a soldier overcame his fear and raised his rifle to stare down the iron sights at the creature. It roared to life and smashed forward, clenching its jaws around his head, shattering his helmet and spraying blood everywhere. Another soldier tried to run, and the Shat let its body carry forward, smashing into him and sending the man flailing across the compound. The woman on top seemed to shift perfectly with the creature, maintaining her balance even as it lurched around with sudden movements. The creature leaned backward and then brought the full force of its body forward, smashing down the rag-doll-limp body it carried onto a frightened soldier. Pinning the man down, its great spider legs flexed inward. The corpse's eyes grew wide as its mouth stretched to unnatural limits and it began devouring the man's face. The rest of the crowd seemed to be able to run past without even a sideways glance from the Shat. Its spider-like body had finally frozen as all of its attention was on the corpse it held. It continued its business of gorging on the twitching soldier.

A short soldier in body armor crept up toward the monster from the side, then rushed in to drag the woman off the creature.

The second she felt her weight shift, Barbie screamed, "No!" and, rolling her shoulder across her side, let her arm fling with a snap. In an instant, she had slashed through the man's neck between his shoulder and head armor with a large, straight-back blade. Arterial blood issued forth. Drops arced forward and sprayed across the Shat's carapace. It twitched and spun abruptly, letting its jaws sever the man's head. The decapitated body stood and twitched a moment before it fell limply to the ground.

Gunfire clacked through the night as one man fired across the clearing toward the Shat. Barbie rolled backward and disappeared off the Shat's body and out of sight in one smooth motion. The Shat leapt in front of one of the partygoers who had frozen up in the line of fire. Bullets struck the corpse's body with loud thunks as the Shat lunged left and right to continue using the corpse as a shield.

Several cameras on stage focused on the soldier as he fumbled with the pouches lining the front of his armor to fetch another magazine. The remaining screens on the Shat zoomed out as it swung its body violently to one side, throwing the corpse into the night.

Its long, spidery legs fluttered and tensed as its pink carapace glowed with a blue hue from the electrical light shining above. The Shat's body folded out, extending a long dragon-like head out from underneath. Two mandibles extended down. Large round globes on the side of its elongated face rotated forward, letting their round expanse ripple. The massive eyelids blinked open. Its head sniffed upward a moment, and its newly opened eyes peered around with wonder as if seeing the night for the first time.

"Make room," Ashley shouted at Mason as she and Donathan climbed onto the picnic table and spun to face the scene playing out in the crowd.

The Shat jolted forward, letting its legs hoist its body high into the air. Its face had soured into a look of rage as it screamed at the sky. A soldier sprinted out of the crowd and, placing one foot forward, raised his barrel and took aim.

The screens behind the stage showed a small hand slowly creeping up over one of his shoulders. In an instant, the hand had unsnapped the man's helmet and ripped it off, showing a man with dark, curly hair staring down the barrel of a rifle. The man's eyes, which had been squinting a second before as he was anticipating the round going off from his steady trigger squeeze, filled with shock as arms suddenly wrapped themselves around his arms and tucked them down to his side, forcing him to drop his rifle. The cameras zoomed in to show Barbie hugging the man tightly from behind. She was either wearing a microphone, or someone had rushed a microphone nearby because her voice rang out as she whispered into the man's ear, "Cry for me."

She spun them both around and took a knee behind him, still clutching the struggling man's arms to his sides. The Shat's posture shifted as it refolded its body in on itself, keeping the two low, pink mandibles forward and revealing a slightly larger, gray mandible above the other two. Its limbs straightened and waved steadily for a moment before snapping down over Barbie's kneeling body and into the back of the man's head. Barbie crawled around to face the man, and all the screens on stage shifted to a side view of her looking up into the twitching man's eyes.

"Stop fighting!" she shouted as she slapped him hard across the face.

The man's arms twitched, and his eyelids flickered.

"I SAID, STOP FUCKING FIGHTING IT!" She slapped the man's head sideways again before he let out a very audible hiss.

Slowly, the man's body turned away before the head swung back around to face Barbie, bobbing slowly as his whole body dangled from the new grip the Shat held on him.

Microphones amplified her laughter as she giggled in an amused tone and said, "Hello, Beauty..." before reaching up and placing her hand upon the man's cheek.

The crowd parted, and Mary Helen stepped out a few hundred yards in front of the two. Her face donned a dark look of fury. She raised one hand and edged it back as if preparing to slap the scene she was witnessing. Then her arm just froze in place, leaving her staring at Barbie and Beauty, waiting for them to make the first move.

Recognizing the dare, Barbie reached down and untucked her knife from her fur leg warmer, then looked up and nodded at the hissing Beauty before she snapped forward into a dead sprint toward Mary Helen. Beauty's legs blurred to life as the Shat galloped behind her, letting the freshly captured man's limbs flail around as the spindly creature ran behind Barbie toward its new prey.

Mary Helen didn't blink. She just continued to stare at her enemy crossing the ground toward her. Finally, in one swift motion she brought her open palm forward, letting her knees drop out from under her and slapping her hand down on the ground. Her shoulders and head seemed to hunch into the motion as she performed it.

The ground shook with force. The screens on stage flickered as one of them snapped off its perch and smashed down, sending plastic and glass across the stage. People screamed and shouted warnings as the crowd fell over each other, trying to reach the edges of the compound where the vehicles were. Small fissures emerged from the ground under Mary Helen's hand and grew into large recesses of concrete as the crevices split open and widened, rushing toward Barbie. Beauty halted and spread its spidery legs across the stable ground to steady itself.

Barbie still rushed forward toward her target, her head low and eyes narrowed with her knife held in her right hand and trailing behind her as she sprinted. The ground fell out from under her.

One of the cameras on stage showed an overhead shot as she spun in midair to look up. As she fell through the crack into the earth and the darkness engulfed her features, a scream of help issued forth in a lone word echoing up from the shadows: "BEAUTY!"

The Shat shivered and then threw its body into the hole after her. Rock and concrete toppled under its spider legs as its pink form vanished out of sight, sliding down the hole after Barbie.

The remaining functional screens on stage focused back on Mary Helen's face. She was standing back up, wind sweeping through her long, jet-black hair. Her eyes focused as a menacing grin crossed her lips.

"Uhh. UHHHH..." Mason stammered, extending one of his hands across the cleared ground, pointing ahead of them toward the dark-haired woman, who was staring at the three of them. She reached back with her right hand and drew a sword that had been slung out of sight on her back, reached across her waist with her left hand and produced a pistol, then walked toward the trio with both weapons hanging low at her sides.

"We need to get the hell out of here," Donathan said in one quick sentence.

"I have a vehicle," a high-pitched voice said in a calm manner.

Donathan, Ashley, and Mason all turned slowly to their left with dumbfounded looks on their faces. Standing on the picnic table next to them was a small girl wearing glasses and a pink knit beanie. She wasn't facing them but was instead staring across the clearing toward Mary Helen's determined pace as if studying her.

"Where the hell did—" Ashley began.

Donathan interrupted, "Car now, questions later," as he extended an arm and shoved everyone back off the picnic table.

The group fell into a dead sprint toward the far side of the compound, opposite where they had come in. The girl with the pink beanie kept the pace without wheezing or gasping for air. Crowds of people were dense here, frantically securing things to vehicles and barking commands and directions for where people should pull up. Once they had reached the center of the vehicles, everyone else seemed winded.

The girl just added, "I'm Nyla, by the way. It's nice to meet you." Then she sprinted past everyone and into a black-and-red Winnebago's side door.

Ashley looked back at her friends, stunned as she gasped for breath, looking flustered. On the side of the vehicle Nyla disappeared into was written one lone word in over-sized Old English lettering: Eniac.

Loudspeakers positioned all around the compound came to life with a woman's voice methodically repeating, "Rally point: Blue."

The three ripped open the door of the Winnebago and rushed inside. Mason stopped mid-step, turned to the rear of the vehicle, and noticed multicolored tags littering the floor, tables, counters, and sink. They were even sticking out of the cabinets, where they were haphazardly wedged. Donathan shoved him forward.

Nyla sat perched in the driver's seat, and Mason rushed to the passenger seat as Ashley and Donathan sat in bench seats behind them.

The woman's voice outside the Winnebago continued repeating, "Rally point: Blue." Inside, it seemed muffled and far off.

Tags fell and shuffled behind them as the Winnebago rumbled to life and lumbered forward through the crowd of vehicles. A man, whose face makeup had been hastily removed, leaving white streaks across his cheeks, and who was wearing a green-and-white jumper, waved his hands and motioned them ahead until they were parked in the front row of vehicles, only a few feet from the electrical pulsing and surging blue-lit fence.

Mason gasped and sat forward up out of his seat to get a better look.

Nyla echoed his enthusiasm and remarked in a spacey tone, "I know, it's brilliant, isn't it?"

Ashley remarked in a more realistic fashion, "How are we going to get out of it?"

Nyla replied, "Well, we could drive through it—"

Donathan sniffed uncomfortably as she said it.

Sensing his apprehension, she replied, "Oh, it's perfectly safe for humans." She grinned over her shoulder for a second, then turned her attention back to the fence. "Its current only kills undead flesh. Well, rips it apart, actually." Her voice sped up into a frenzy. "It really is an amazing creation. Zombies seem to be able to sense it, though, and most usually give it a pretty wide berth. But it is perfectly safe for humans. You can walk through it and only feel a small tickle. Although if we drove through it, our vehicle would definitely stop working—"

"So *how* are we going to get through it?" Ashley asked.

"Oh, the failsafe!" Nyla's tone rose in an excited manner. "It's quite unique. They should be firing it off any minute—"

A loud explosion rumbled from behind the Winnebago, and engines from vehicles around them revved. A second explosion rang through the night, and Nyla remarked, "It won't be long now!" as she pressed her body forward against the windshield of the Winnebago and looked up into the sky.

Mason looked confused and edged forward again, peering up and trying to see what she was staring at. A third explosion sounded, its blast much closer than the previous three. Hot glowing red metal showered away from the compound, falling to the earth on the other side of the electric fence. Its glowing embers dropped into parts of the abandoned city and the desert ahead of the Winnebago. The fence flickered as a fourth explosion sounded and the coils violently flung forward away from the vehicle. Their masses twisted and untangled as they extended across the ground ahead. One final buzz sounded before the blue glow faded from the wires and a small purple Volkswagen bug darted out across the cables toward the horizon. A loud roar erupted as vehicles all jammed their accelerators down and the line of cars surged forward.

Nyla was laughing and shouting about a perfect execution as the Winnebago matched the trajectory of the other automobiles and angled itself onto the dusty open road toward the desert sun's rays, just starting to peek out over the dark indigo skyline.

STEVEN MIX

17.

Heading North on Shytown Trail

Zombie Civil Rights Group

Present Day

THE ROAD HAD NARROWED. Nyla calmed down to near silence after the initial excitement of escaping the festival. Shortly after they managed to get on the road, Ashley asked where they were headed, and Nyla replied in an informative voice, "We have to head to the rally point, which is the lady in Santa Clara." As the day progressed, vehicle after vehicle kept peeling off from the crowd, either speeding ahead or taking different routes, until only the Winnebago remained.

The previous night had worn on the group. About mid-afternoon, Donathan managed to wander around the back cabin until he found a bed and shoved all of the multicolored tags off of it, sending them scattering them across the floor. Ashley was still sitting on the cushioned bench facing a mounted table behind the driver's seat, but she was facedown with her arms wrapped around her head, fast asleep.

The Winnebago's brakes squeaked slightly as it rumbled to a stop, forcing tags to shift from their resting places as the whole cabin rocked forward. Nyla turned the key, pocketed it, and stood up, still facing the window, before she sighed and turned around, raising one of her eyebrows quizzically.

In the back of the cabin, Mason stepped away from his current work. A large tornado of red and black tags, overlapping and swirling, frozen in time, were sprawled across the back wall, spreading their faux chaos fluidly over the cabinets and counters and down the plastic molding until the cyclone dwindled and narrowed, disappearing into the floor. One small space near the center of the scene showed part of a wooden cabinet. Looking guilty, Mason lowered his head, still holding an oversized bottle of wood glue in one hand and a red tag in the other.

"I'm sorry," he managed to mumble in a tone heavy with regret as his left arm slowly raised itself toward the tip of the wood glue bottle and then, as if moving with a mind of its own, flailed to his left, covering the hole in the twister and gluing the last tag to the cabinet.

"Goodness," Nyla exclaimed. After a moment of silence, she added, "Could you do something similar on the outside of the Eniac?"

"Don't encourage him," Ashley croaked, stirring in her arms and slowly raising her head. "Ever." Her hair was disheveled, strands strewn all over her face. She sniffed quietly before adding, "I'm hungry."

Nyla nodded and said, "Well, I have some twenty-year-old cereal in one of the cabinets." She paused, looking up in a thoughtful manner. "Or I could pan sear an artichoke and sauté it in a lemon-pepper-and-honey glaze until it's golden brown around the edges and serve it up with a Dijon paste I've perfected over the last few years."

Ashley sat up suddenly but kept her neck stiff and both of her eyes forward, out of focus and distant. In an abnormally calm tone, she said, "That'd be fine."

Nyla nodded, gathered a few items from a cabinet below the sink, and then stepped out the door of the Winnebago, letting light scatter inside for a moment.

Mason had already rushed forward from the back of the camper, leaving the bottle of wood glue on a counter in the back. "What the hell is an artich—"

"Don't you ruin this for me," Ashley said in an icy tone, narrowing her eyes and poking an accusing finger at his face.

After a few minutes, Nyla returned and set down on the table a saucer with a leafy green vegetable that had been halved and well cooked. She placed a small wooden bowl filled with a light-maize-colored paste next to it.

Both Ashley and Mason stared down at all the leaves, wearing confused looks until Nyla picked up on their hesitation, reached down, peeled off one of the leaves, and then slid the husk-edged side through the Dijon before raising it to chew off the pulp hanging on the other side of the leaf.

Ashley was the first to try it, and the moment the artichoke leaf passed her lips, her eyes drifted shut, and a sigh of elation and wonder filled the cramped cabin. Mason followed suit with a similar result, and they gasped and shoved for the next five minutes over the remainder of leaves.

Donathan finally stirred and sat up from the bed asking, "Where are we?" Dark circles under his eyes gave away the fact he hadn't actually slept much.

"Technically only a few hours north of Clovis." Nyla paused for a moment to gather her thoughts before continuing in a dazed manner, "The roads are absolute nightmares around here." She giggled slightly before adding, "But so is the nightlife."

Ashley looked up curiously at Nyla, pausing from ravenously devouring the artichoke, before shrugging and hunching back over to continue shoveling in food. Mason hadn't stopped.

Donathan slid his feet around and let his boots thump down onto the floor of the vehicle before finally edging his eyes back up toward Nyla, and his smile fell into its usual rhythm. "Why are we stopping here, then? Shouldn't we be making our way to an enclave?"

Nyla shook her head slightly and readjusted her glasses before speaking. "It's far safer on this stretch of the trail to make camp away from the enclaves. There's too many Falling Sands loyalists here who don't trust strangers." Nyla turned in a dazed manner and strolled out the door of the camper.

"I hate playing sundown hide-n-seek," Donathan mumbled before standing.

Mason and Ashley just grunted with mouthfuls of food in response. Walking past the duo, Donathan said sarcastically, "Don't get up," then turned and exited through the mobile home's door.

Pausing to let his eyes adjust to the sudden shock of the bright day, Donathan finally spied Nyla tugging at and picking through a pile of electrical cords hanging outside a large compartment near one of the tire wells. He rushed over and helped her through the process of separating the tangle of cables. Eventually, she pulled aside a large orange cable with bare copper wiring extending several feet on one end, braided into a metal ring with a large round orb attached.

Nyla carelessly shoved all the other cords back into the compartment and tried unsuccessfully several times to close it. When she finally managed to get it latched, she sat back a moment, drew a deep breath and added, "Science is a beast in and of itself."

Donathan's smile flashed off as he appreciated the sudden, deep comment that issued forth from the tiny blonde girl across from him.

When his smile returned, he said, "Look, I don't mean to question your usual routine, but camping here past sundown seems like a foolish move." Nyla had already opened another compartment next to the first and was fishing through various objects. Donathan continued, "I know the sun's going down, but perhaps if we just kept moving in the RV, we might make it to—"

"Aha!" Nyla shouted, holding up two spikes with leather straps attached to them. Donathan stepped back defensively after her semi-maniacal outburst. "They're always so hard to find! Today was simple!" She seemed to be steadily growing wild-eyed as the words hurried out of her.

Donathan stood up a little straighter, stretched, and finally sighed, figuring it was unavoidable. "Okay... so what are those for?"

"For climbing, of course." Nyla had sat down and begun lashing them to her ankles.

Donathan looked confused. "Of course? What are we climbing?"

It was Nyla's turn to look confused as she finished fastening the straps. "Power poles. How else are we going to get power?"

Donathan finally gave up trying to figure out just what she was doing and helped her back to her feet, and she hoisted the end of the cable with the orb over a shoulder and sauntered across the road, bowlegged with the metal spikes dragging from her insteps. The other end of the cable trailed back into that compartment on the Winnebago. When she finally reached an old wooden power pole, she stepped up and slammed the arch of her foot into the pole, securing the spike into its wooden bark before raising her other foot six inches higher and doing the same. Once she was roughly seven feet up, she reached an arm above her head and secured the first steel handhold in a series jutting out from the pole and used those to raise herself higher. After her feet made it to the steel handholds, she placed the toes of her feet on those to climb. She continued this process up the power pole, only pausing once to readjust the cable hanging over her shoulder.

When she was just below the power coupling with stretched wires overhead, she shrugged her shoulders and with one arm tugged the coil of her own wires over her head. Taking hold of the orbed end, she let the rest of the copper and orange cable elongate below her before swinging back. Letting its momentum carry forward, she swung her arm up and toward the coupling, loosening her grasp and letting the orb slide out of her hand to carry the flowing copper wire, trailing behind it as it arced over her head. Without waiting for the round orb to finish falling, Nyla very quickly scaled down the pole.

In an instant, a loud pop and a pulsing sound could be heard as the copper cables settled over the power lines and coupling, using the orb as a counterweight. The orb began to glow and pulse with dim blue streaks of electricity.

Nyla had already reached the ground when mechanical sounds emanated from the Winnebago. Donathan spun around to face its whirs and buzzes.

Along the top edges of the vehicle's frame, small black plastic mounts rose up, each with two round inch-sized holes equally spaced across their rectangular faces.

"The whole Shytown Trail has active power poles. Well, most of it anyway. Many enclaves don't tap into it, for fear of being targeted by the Protectorate."

Nyla cleared her throat as Ashley and Mason emerged from the Winnebago with a small slam of the vehicle's door as if to announce their presence. Nyla's tone became a bit serious as she said, "Once the Protectorate has sent representatives from Falling Sands, most people or enclaves don't hold out very long. Most of the trail won't trade with that enclave, and then the Protectorate Army arrives and..." Nyla trailed off.

Ashley shot a concerned glance to Donathan, who was still half smiling, then back toward Mason. She sighed and then scratched at the scar on her cheek before asking, "Has anyone ever fought the Protectorate Army and won?"

Nyla shrugged, "No. I don't think so. No one alive. They've been beaten by the undead before, but that's why they live where they live."

It was Donathan's turn to be curious. "What do you mean?"

Nyla crossed past the group, opened the door to the Winnebago, reached inside, and opened a small compartment right alongside the doorframe before turning back to face the three friends. "Well, zombies don't go three places in California." She then asked in a concerned voice, "Can you all step a little closer?"

Ashley stepped toward Nyla, and a moment later, Donathan and Mason did the same. Nyla flipped a switch, and a very quiet hum rose from the Winnebago.

Nyla shut the compartment, closed the door, and stepped back up to the rest of the group. "Unless forced, the undead won't go to Half Moon Bay, Falling Sands, or Oakland." The hum was quite a bit louder. "I don't know why they don't go to Half Moon Bay. Perhaps because of the density of salt water in the air there, or perhaps because of the climate. Unless coaxed, they just stay away from Half Moon Bay. Falling Sands they avoid because of all the harvester enclaves on the edges of it; most zombies won't make it anywhere near Falling Sands unless they're inside a trade caravan."

"And Oakland?" Mason asked.

The hum grew quiet, and each of the plastic mounts on the top of the Winnebago fired two thin cable wires from their holes, angled so they fired into the ground all around the clearing. Mason jumped as several fired over the heads of the group and into the dirt behind them.

Nyla's shoulders hunched forward. "Zombies don't go to Oakland"—she drew a breath before whispering in a serious manner—"because Oakland can defend itself."

As the last syllable faded away, blue tendrils of current pulsed into existence across the wires above, letting their electrical trails surge and hop from one wire to the next. Their new compound glowed azure in the fading sunlight.

Ashley looked dumbfounded. "You have the same technology as the Knight's Moon?"

Nyla nodded and strolled past them, toward the back of the vehicle. "Of course," she called out as she rounded the back of the Winnebago. "I designed it."

Ashley looked at Donathan, who shrugged, then back to Mason and followed after Nyla. Nyla was struggling with another compartment, trying to force it open. Donathan stepped forward and grasped the handle for her, giving it a good, quick yank. With a pop, the compartment opened and a great deal of objects dropped out, causing Donathan and Nyla to quickly step back.

As the dust settled, Ashley chirped in shock, "She has treasure!" She quickly reached down and secured a guitar from the pile. Donathan had swooped up another guitar and sauntered back around the corner of the RV. Mason picked through the pile, shoving away a banjo and another guitar before picking up a French horn, raising it to head height, and staring at it curiously.

Ashley rested her right hand across the strings and let her left extend down the neck of the guitar and back up for a moment, allowing the texture of the wood to slide through her palm as her fingers flexed. Drawing in a slow breath, her eyes drooped slightly as the fingers on both her hands strummed and slid at the same time with deft control. Fingers became small blurs as the picking of a flamenco tune flowed out from the guitar, leaving notes to hang thick in the air.

Nyla had been studying Ashley's hands intently and slowly reached down, dragging a guitar up from the pile. Carefully, she raised the strap over her head, letting it rest on one shoulder, then stood next to Ashley, who had shut her eyes at this point. Nyla let her shoulders slump slightly to match Ashley's posture, and after a moment more of intense staring, she played her guitar to match Ashley's rhythm and tune perfectly.

Ashley's eyes shot open, and she gave Nyla a sideways glance before asking over the music, "You know how to play flamenco?"

Nyla shrugged and replied, "I guess so."

Ashley continued strumming the guitar a moment, then sang the lyrics to Afrika Bambaataa's "Planet Rock" over the music as she walked away. Nyla's strumming slowed and halted as she wondered out loud, "Did I do something wrong?"

Mason added, "She's not used to being shown up." He was standing up empty-handed and walked back toward the rest of the group.

"Do you not know how to play an instrument?" Nyla asked in her usual voice.

Mason nodded, "Donathan always made sure we practiced when they were available. Music and rhythm go hand in hand with the dance of combat. That's what he said, anyways." Mason motioned toward the sound around the corner, "They certainly love it, but it's not really my... medium."

Nyla had taken off the guitar and let it rest back on the pile of musical instruments, pausing a second before strolling back around the corner of the RV. Then over her shoulder, she said, "I have art supplies—well, paint anyways."

Mason managed to trip and fall over without actually walking anywhere. He rushed to his feet and sprinted after her around the corner.

Donathan and Ashley were sitting cross-legged across from each other near the middle of the campsite laughing, strumming the guitars with determination, and bouncing different melodies off each other, occasionally singing vocals over the tunes.

Nyla had already opened another compartment, this one perched near the back tire well, and reached in to produce several spray cans, red, blue, and gray, which she tried to tuck into her arms to turn to hand to Mason, but he had already rushed forward and started picking them from her arms.

Nyla looked at Mason and said, "You're welcome to the others in there—"

Mason shoved her aside and feverishly fished more spray cans out of the dark cubby, and Nyla turned to walk away saying, "Goodness!" She rubbed the dust off one of her hands onto her white t-shirt then reached up to readjust her glasses before walking toward Donathan and Ashley.

An unearthly scream erupted from the tree line. Ashley threw down the guitar and drew her bat while Donathan stood up stunned and spun around to face the zombie's screaming. Ball bearings clacked on metal as paint cans fell.

The sky was still dim with orange overhead contrasting off the blue electricity surrounding the clearing.

Ashley and Donathan backed up toward the RV and finally laid eyes on the creature near the power pole outside of the compound. Two legs and one arm held it low to the ground. One arm was snaked up under it, the other one missing entirely. It stood, letting a few strands of long hair dangle down as it kneeled in the dirt. After a moment, it screamed again, arching its back and letting its contorted face rage toward the sky. Rotten, gray flesh showered forward as the flood of sound and anguish faded away, and in an instant it was on its feet sprinting toward the living.

Nyla had her hands behind her back, her shoulders squared as she calmly stepped up next to Ashley. "Oh, my," she said enthusiastically. "One of the Cacophony."

In an instant, the fence line surged as the undead charged through the blue electricity and, smoking lightly, flexed its legs for a moment, then leapt ferociously toward Donathan. Ashley put a determined step between them at the last second and swung the bat in a fast one-handed flick, connecting with its face. Ashley and Donathan were suddenly covered in smoke, dust, and embers as the zombie's entire body ashed away.

Donathan and Ashley coughed and sputtered as Nyla stood only three feet away, completely smudge-free. Nyla chirped, pleased for a moment before adding, "A perfect execution every time."

Ashley was trying to shake the blackened soot from her hair and was half glaring at Nyla as Nyla walked away and said, "I must go tagging."

Mason dropped the last spray can he was holding.

18.

North on Shytown Trail

Zombie Civil Rights Group

Present Day

NYLA RE-EMERGED FROM THE WINNEBAGO, wearing a small backpack with a water tube draped up and over one shoulder. Her arms strained as she held a mass of rifles in them, her hands curled up over the front toward her chin. After a half hour of reassurances that they would be fine, she managed to get everyone to take the weapons she had produced and step through the tingling blue tendrils of electricity. When they all finally made it through, Nyla set down her rifle, turned on a small L-shaped red flashlight, and attached it to the front shoulder strap of her backpack while explaining, "Red light is quite subdued. The military used it before the undead destroyed most of the nation," in her best matter-of-fact voice.

She produced a small parchment from her pants pocket, unfolded it, and stared down at it for a moment before explaining they should follow a ridgeline until it crossed a stream and should make sure not to head any further east because there were Burrowers.

"What's a Burrower?" Donathan had asked curiously.

Nyla winced and said, "It's best if you never find out. They aren't really common, so just stay out of their territory."

After an hour of walking, they made their way toward the top of the ridge. About halfway up, Nyla's flashlight pulsed extremely bright for a moment in three short bursts. Nyla swore loudly and then sprinted up the ridge.

Everyone had frozen in shock at hearing her voice take on such a serious tone. When everyone got to the top of the ridge, they could see what Nyla was cursing. Across the valley were three bright, pulsing balls of white light. The orbs were small and distant but clearly on a collision course with them.

"Other travelers?" Ashley questioned with a whisper and bated breath.

The red hue of the light showed Nyla's frown in the dark night. "Far worse... Shocks."

Donathan cleared his throat nervously, and Nyla picked up on the cue and added, "They already know we're here. I've made a..."—she sighed nervously—"a tactical error bringing us out tonight. They're not supposed to be anywhere near this part of California this time of year. They've sensed my camp and are making a run toward it."

Mason shifted nervously and placed a hand across the buttstock of his rifle.

Donathan asked, "Is the camp safe?"

Nyla nodded. "The system will work perfectly and destroy the Shocks no matter how much charge they put out. They're drawn to it, like a moth to flame. They're the only ones who can sense where the system is when it powers up, and they almost always rush it."

Ashley said in a determined voice, "Then we run for it and—"

Nyla cut her off. "There's no time; our only chance is there." She pointed down to the ridge's base where a small, slow-moving river curled toward and then away from the mountainside. "Even if we tried to get out of their path, they'd probably find us."

Ashley had already thrown her backpack down ahead of her and begun running down the mountain toward it, and Mason quietly quoted an old video game, "What a horrible night... to have a curse."

Small electrical storms surged in patches and danced across the skin of the three undead as they glided across the land. Small trees and bushes whipped in their passage through the night. The fat one led the way with the other two floating strategically to his left and right as they skimmed across the land and lit up the night. Their hands hung at their sides, palms open and facing forward, their feet dangling below them. As they slid along a foot above the ground, the pop and fizz of static could be heard over their low, unearthly groans. Every so often, a large bolt of electricity would drape across their path, angling a large, thick, bright haze of current out and away from them until it vanished in a sudden pop. The fat one slowed to a halt and drifted down to the ground, and his two comrades followed suit.

As he looked back, the jowls on his face shook as he hissed and groaned before facing forward and limping along the sandy bank and into the river. The small arrowhead formation of undead trudged slowly through the water, reeds, and muck. The half moon hung near the horizon as the gentle sloshing sounds of shuffling and water shifted forward through the night.

Mason felt the water before he heard it move and knew the Shocks were coming near. His mask, with the picture of a goldfish swimming in a sea of blue, was pulled down, covering the part of his face not submerged in the river. Floating in the river on his back, he could see everything through the holes of the mask: the stars, the bank leading up the side of the mountain, and his three friends floating in the river around him. All of their feet were pointed toward each other, and in the light of the moon, Mason could even see their faces as the water churned slightly around them. The first zombie stalked past them, its bulbous legs causing the water to splash and cascade around its legs. Ashley could feel the water shifting behind her and was staring past Mason, wild eyed, her mouth just under the water's edge. The water shook violently as another zombie sauntered past, its head black with one eye dangling from its socket. Strings from a t-shirt that had long since been shredded hung down from its torso and drifted through the water alongside him. Only a second had passed before another zombie crossed into Mason's field of vision and halted. The water's movement slowed, and Mason could hear a light trickling noise as it turned and slowly faced the group of humans hiding in the shadowy water of the river. The undead swayed a moment as if taking in the scene, and Mason turned his head to his left as Nyla shifted, her body still bathed in water, and brought a hand up toward her cheek and waved cheerfully at the zombie.

Mason's heart skipped a beat as a screech rose up from the river and the zombie hissed, baring its teeth. Electrical pulses propagated across its cheeks and spread down its neck as it took one final step toward them. For a moment, everyone in the river shuddered as the water was bombarded with electricity.

A large splash erupted from the water as the Shock fell backward. A second later, it stumbled to its feet, groaned at the group, and then fell forward before limping ahead on its path after its undead kin.

Two minutes later, when Nyla stood up in the two-foot-deep water, Ashley stuck her head up and gasped, "Holy living fuck."

Nyla chimed in, "Yes. Shocks can't charge up in water. It hurts them more than it hurts us..."

"Why didn't they just wait us out?" Donathan asked while trying to get to his feet, water cascading off his shoulders.

"I don't think they stop moving much at all when they're awake." Nyla's voice had a sense of wonderment to it. "During the day, they sleep in whatever shade or abandoned building they can find, but I've never seen them stop for longer than thirty seconds at night." She shrugged before adding, "They are pretty active at sundown, though."

After they made their way out of the river, they walked along the bank, paralleling the ridgeline and making their way back to the compound.

After fifty minutes of walking, the haze of the camp-site could be seen just over the ridge. Mason halted behind them and pointed just across the river, "There's a shack over there." A tiny four-walled shack stood ominously in the darkness with one lone window facing their direction. Broken chunks of shingles from the disheveled roof lay all along the riverbank's edge.

Nyla made an excited squeal, pulled a wet piece of parchment out of her pocket, checked it, and nodded. "Perfect! That's the perfect place to tag!"

Ashley just shrugged at Donathan, who replied, "Why don't we stay here?"

Mason was already sending water spraying through the night as he stumbled and sprinted through the river toward the other side. Nyla was following close behind. Once they'd reached the other side, Nyla had shut off her light, slung her rifle onto her back, and managed to crawl in behind him, causing the old wood from below the window to creak a bit. Mason paused to dig through his backpack and find a red spray can before swinging his rifle through the frame of the window and into the darkness inside the shack. The sound of a spray can broke the quietness, and fumes filled the air. After a few quick bursts from the spray can, a growl echoed up from inside the house, and the spraying stopped.

A second later, the inside of the house lit up from the dull glow of the Zippo lighter Nyla was holding in her left hand. Mason was still facing the wall and holding a spray can aloft in his right hand, where he had been halted mid-spray. His rifle was propped up against the wall next to him. The letters Z, C, and half an R had been outlined on the wall before him, and red paint trailed down the plywood. His mouth was open, and a look of horror seemed to be screaming from his eyes as he stared down his nose at the scene in front of him. Standing directly in front of Nyla was a burly, thick-armed, gaunt-eyed undead with dark green scales stretching across his face. One of its ears was ripped and hung loosely on its left side.

Nyla shifted the Zippo forward and let it come to rest just inches from the center of his face.

In return, the monster hissed and stared cross-eyed at the flame.

In a soothing voice, Nyla hushed it, saying slowly, "It's... okay... You're fine..." She had been fishing through her pockets and finally produced a small blue tag. She reached up and bit down on the tag, holding it between her teeth before swapping hands, juggling the lighter to her other hand. She removed the tag and, still making slight shushing noises, reached up toward the zombie's ear. As she grasped the lobe, it fell off into her hand.

"Oh bother," Nyla remarked in an absentminded voice. All at once, the zombie reared back and screeched, and two large, dark-green limbs jolted out from behind its back and swayed in the darkness, aimed directly at Nyla's head. The zombie gnashed its teeth toward the flickering flame with the clack of a seasoned predator.

Without hesitation, Nyla snapped part of the tag through the ear and reached up, jamming it into the mouth of the undead. A look of confusion and disgust crossed its eyes as it swallowed its own ear.

"Whhhat the ffff—" Mason snatched up his rifle and dove out the window. He was halfway across the river and could hear Nyla floundering behind him as the wall of the shack shattered, sending splinters ahead of them through the night.

Muzzles flashed and bullets whizzed past them, fired by Donathan and Ashley along with a stream of curse words. The hollow thud of flesh and scales being impacted by round after round echoed up through the night. A vicious scream ripped through the night, and Mason sprinted past his friends and up ahead toward the compound, not pausing to look back and engage the monster. The sound of gunfire faded away as everyone else did the same. Branches could be heard snapping behind the group as the creature loped after them.

Mason ran through the blue electricity and into the safety of the compound before turning to see Ashley and Nyla sprint through behind him. The electrical current seemed to part as Donathan dove through headfirst and landed hard on his left shoulder, losing grip on his rifle. The large, muscled form of the tailed zombie silhouetted in the live current of the blue fence line.

Electricity surged as the undead broke through the current, ripping one of the lines from the ground and causing it to snap back across the clearing toward the RV. The zombie vanished in a puff of smoke and blackened soot that filled the gap made by the missing line.

Covered in ashes, Donathan opened his pale eyes and coughed on the ground, trying to shake the ruins and embers free. "I'm tired of feeling like an ash tray," he wheezed.

"What the fuck?" Ashley screamed.

Nyla took another moment to catch her breath, reached into her pants pocket, pulled out and held up a plastic tag, and then shrugged while saying in a calm voice, "I told you... I was going tagging."

19.

Santa Clara

Zombie Civil Rights Group

Present Day

THE WINNEBAGO LUMBERED into Santa Clara just after nine in the morning. Ashley turned and angled the large RV down a road, passing an occasional rusty green street sign that said Bowers. Most of the houses in this area had fallen into disarray. Many of the neighborhoods were pockmarked with caved-in rooftops, fallen picket fences, and blackened masses of ash where walls once stood, and all that remained was the concrete foundation. The world here seemed lost in a moment of destruction. No one had ever bothered to rebuild here.

"There's probably not an enclave for fifty miles," Ashley commented quietly to herself as she turned the wheel to find a path around some rubble in the two-lane road.

Inside the Eniac was a far different atmosphere. Hip-hop beats quietly trickled out of the speakers that Nyla had jury-rigged. She had found them in one of the outside compartments and mounted them in corners of the vehicle's ceiling two days back. Donathan had commandeered the bed again, and Nyla was fast asleep on the floor. Mason sat in the booth, head lowered so one of his cheeks was resting on the tabletop as his eyes followed the tip of a pencil shading patterns across the shiny, flat surface he was resting against.

They had been traveling north for just over three days, picking their path slowly through rubble and streets that had long been forgotten. Several times, they had to backtrack to find a new path, and each time Nyla quietly commented on how the roads up north needed to be remapped. Eventually, she had decided that she would take the problem on herself during her next trip. Their slow travel speed wasn't helped by the fact that the RV moved as slow as a boat, but as long as they traveled on the roads by day, set up camp at night, and took efforts to avoid major enclaves, the world had begun to feel less tense and horror-filled.

Nyla still disappeared every night to go "tagging," but everyone else was resigned to let her go by herself after the first night's adventure. Mason looked terribly concerned each night she crept out toward the blue light of the cable's fence line, and twice Ashley reminded him that she had been doing this for some time and that everyone else was not as good as her at night. Nyla stopped one night and turned around to smile back at Ashley as if agreeing.

None of this stopped Nyla from educating the group on the various maps she had created of the "migratory patterns of the modern Californian zombie." At sunset each day, when the compound was set up, Nyla would spread sheets in the dust and sand and talk to the wide-eyed Ashley and Donathan about the different breeds of undead and what the various symbols and keys of the maps meant. Mason's mind would usually drift off to something else, and the only real knowledge he ever retained was the fact that you always stayed out of the vertical-line-shaded areas she had marked. Nyla also showed them how to spot gas stations that still might have untouched storage tanks, how to gain access to them, and how to siphon gas from abandoned vehicles that were "strategically marked and refilled" by the Knight's Moon.

Aside from the occasional flash of light and ash-strewing entrance to their campsites, Donathan, Ashley, and Mason hadn't even seen a zombie for a few days. They learned to hang out closer to the RV when setting up and once even fell asleep under the stars to the gentle pop and hiss of a campfire while the darkness roamed safely away from them.

Only one of the nights did Nyla rush back ahead of an undead who charged to its death behind her. Most of the time, she arrived quietly and retired into the camper, and everyone else would let her sleep in a bit as they took down the campsite, packed up, and prepared to head out each day. Even Ashley let her guard down long enough to become friends with Nyla, laughing and joking inside the camper about artichokes and tales of Mason's art projects, as well as the running joke of the Puppy Suit.

Four days after they fled the Knight's Moon festival, Ashley cut the wheel to pull around a mass of ripped and piled tires in the road as she angled the vehicle up an overpass that led them above old Highway 101. As the RV reached the top and leveled out to face down the hill, she jammed on the brakes with full force, creating a nasty screech of rubber and asphalt. All at once, tags fell and scattered while Donathan lunged to his feet shouting gibberish and Nyla started awake behind the driver's seat saying, "Goodness!"

Ashley jumped up out of the seat, turned to face her friends, and announced with excitement, "We're here."

The door to the RV banged shut, and Mason took a deep breath while he surveyed the scene below him. Sounds of laughter and excited shouts rang up at them, and for a moment he had to just stand and blink in the rising morning sun. "What am I looking at?" he finally asked.

Nyla replied with her usual spacey voice, "The Lady of Santa Clara, of course…" She paused mid-sentence to look back down the road toward the small valley ahead of them. "And the Knight's Moon, of course. Remember I told you this was the rally point?"

Large coil wires of Nyla's design ran off poles towering high above massive groups of people. Canvas tents painted with designs lined the ground and spread out across both concrete roads and dirt paths stretching toward the horizon. People could be seen emerging from them and rushing about, performing their assigned tasks. Crowds were dense here. It seemed the Knight's Moon never traveled light. The roller coasters of a long-since-abandoned amusement park were framed in the distance on the far right side of their vision, edging behind a few crumbling, and ancient, corporate high-rises. Some of the buildings nearest the encampment had tiny and colorfully clothed individuals entering and exiting them with a sense of purpose. In the dead center of all this action stood a robed silver-and-steel statue of a woman with arms outstretched and her head tilted in a warm and welcoming way.

"I believe she was a religious icon before the world started to crumble. Now she's our first rally point when things don't go according to plan—"

"She's beautiful," Donathan interrupted.

Nyla looked again toward the valley as if seeing it for the first time, then grinned and added, "Yes, I suppose she is."

They made their way down the hill and toward the center of the mishmash of people. Nyla insisted they weren't celebrating—they were just refitting before they made their way to another festival locale—even though they kept passing booths selling barbequed food, beer, and brightly colored clothing. The safety and peace of mind provided by Nyla's inventions extended throughout the Knight's Moon followers. She was recognized occasionally as they walked along, and people would rush forward and offer her free skewered meat or shake her hand and thank her. Each time, Nyla would shyly nod and look as if she dreaded this sort of interaction. The first time it happened, Ashley paused and gave her a long, confused look. Whenever people walked away, Nyla would sheepishly offer Ashley, Donathan, and Mason the food she was given. A long string of thank-yous would issue forth, followed by the three of them stuffing their cheeks far more voraciously than any undead feeding.

When they finally made it to the feet of the statue, everyone had a full belly, and the sun hung high in the air.

Mason leaned his shoulders back, looked up at the top of the statue, and said in an overwhelmed voice, "I... art..."

Ashley shot a confused look at him and then back to Donathan, who just shrugged his shoulders.

"Well, well, well..."

Ashley spun around to find herself standing a few feet away from Paul, one of the hosts of the Knight's Moon. Ginn was nowhere to be seen.

Paul's tired eyes blinked from the handle of her baseball bat appearing over her shoulder from where it hung strapped to her back, back to the center of Ashley's face while he added, "Look what the bat dragged in..."

As if annoyed at his own comment, he sighed, looked up at the bright sun then back down at Ashley before projecting in a loud voice, "Nyla, be a dear and check the third and fifth generators. They were making a terrible ruckus last night..."

A sound of acknowledgement came up from behind the group as Nyla rushed off around the statue and vanished out of sight toward a small three-story building.

"Your things have been moved to my chariot and guarded by us personally, as requested by Waterfalz. She seems to think you're important to us."

An uncomfortable silence crept in before Ashley added, "Thank you?" in a quiet voice.

"She also said you're not here for a job, that..."—Paul looked far less amused—"we should give you whatever support you need."

Donathan asked, "Can we meet with her again?"

Paul stood tall, and confidence suddenly oozed from his voice as if he were once again standing on stage. "Afraid *not*, friends. Our sage needs her beauty sleep, and you need... some new color." He stamped one of his feet and then slowly raised one of his hands straight up into the air and lowered it, flexing and extending his arm to two tents behind Donathan. "Tell them Paul sent you and that you need to be 'all themed up.' He'll know what I mean."

Paul's energy lowered a moment, and he asked calmly, "If I may be so bold as to wonder, what's the next stop for you all?"

Plain-faced, Mason spoke first, "Well, Nyla says we need to stop by her old enclave in Half Moon Bay, and besides, we're still looking for the Princess."

Another uncomfortable silence crept in as Paul shot Mason a wide-eyed glance and then whistled a tune, carrying one of the notes out in a long melodious way, and then slowly walked off.

Ashley smacked the back of Mason's head, sending his mask toppling to the ground. "Good job. Now he thinks we're hella weird."

Mason bent over to pick up his mask and then fell forward as the ground shook. Stumbling back to his feet, he made a shocked chirping noise as his eyes focused on the long- and spindly-legged Shat that had landed next to the statue. Barbie, wearing jeans, a light blue tank top, and no shoes, slid down off its pink carapace and cupped her hands in front of her face, lighting a cigarette. Her eyes glazed over and then shut as she drew in a deep breath. Beauty's body still held the armored soldier in front, his limbs hanging free and his hair matted and blackened with dirt and soot. The Shat made a growling noise before pulling its legs in slowly and letting its main body drift down to the ground, resting the soldier's body in front of it, his limbs drifting down to the ground and lying without care or conscious effort like a forgotten rag doll. Most of the crowd rushing around didn't seem to pay any mind to the giant, spider-like undead and its companion, resting next to the Lady of Santa Clara.

Donathan took a step forward and said in Barbie's direction, "We thought for sure you were done for that night."

Barbie didn't acknowledge the words much beyond a far-off stare and an amused "Huh."

Donathan added, "Glad to see you're okay."

Barbie took another drag on her cigarette.

Finally Ashley spoke, "Maybe we should go find Nyla—"

Barbie turned her head quickly and let her eyes drift up and down Ashley's form slowly before staring directly into Ashley's eyes and giving her a slight smile.

Ashley blushed a moment and looked away uncomfortably before Mason took a few steps forward, cautiously reaching a hand toward one of Beauty's legs and adding, "I love your pet."

Beauty leapt up and spun around to face Mason, two legs high and curled overhead, two more legs just under those curled around the dangling soldier, who was hissing, his face contorted. Mason had frozen, wide-eyed, his arm still extended in the air. A moment later, the hissing soldier was edged forward until his face was only an inch away from Mason's fear-filled, frozen visage.

Barbie leaned her head in and whispered, "She's upset... You see, you've gotten it backward. She's not my pet."

Stepping back, Barbie stamped out her cigarette and then in one swift movement leapt up onto Beauty's pink carapace. The creature rose up, stretching its long, rosy limbs and shaking the rag doll it held, and then let out a roar, leaping up onto the chest of the Lady of Santa Clara, stalking up the statue's torso and then onto one of her arms before stretching her giant legs down, then springing up and back out of sight.

"Well…" Donathan said, motioning to the tents that Paul had originally directed them to.

Donathan stepped out first, his brown duster replaced with a black one. The leather smelled new, and although it was not worn in yet, it hung just loose enough that he felt comfortable.

Donathan stretched and then managed to bum a cigarette off of a random Knight's Moon employee who was helping another carry a jackhammer. Once it was lit, Donathan drew in a deep drag and let the taste of nicotine and smoke linger in his mouth and lungs, appreciating how relaxed the day seemed, before finally exhaling.

Paul could be heard shouting over the crowd, demanding that all concrete, from road to sidewalk, be removed by dawn. He added more emphasis to his statement by shouting that things should be "static, people, static!"

Mason stepped out from the same tent Donathan had been in, fussing with his machine gun and how it was slung. Mason was wearing a pair of black jeans, and the camo on his IBA vest had all the desert brown repainted with various shades of red. When he'd finally stopped messing with his weapon's sling, he looked up, locked eyes with Donathan, burst out laughing, and pointed at his own feet. His sneakers were all black with three red stripes. "They had them!" Mason said enthusiastically. "It was almost like they were waiting for me! I didn't even know they came in red and black!"

The curtain stirred on Ashley's tent, and she stepped out.

Donathan's cigarette fell out of his mouth, and Mason looked stunned.

"Well?" Ashley asked.

Ashley was wearing a dark gray, almost black top that buttoned up the middle and had sleeves that extended down her arm just past the shoulder and flared out slightly. Her purple dress had been replaced by one of a similar design except slightly longer and having the same blend of black into color the last one had, except instead of purple, the tones were magenta and red. The most striking thing was a pair of white fingerless batting gloves on her hands. The gloves had red silk scarves lashed and intertwined around her knuckles and wrapped in cross patterns to just past her wrists, where they were tied, leaving cloth flaring out slightly.

"You look amazing," Donathan added. Ashley looked uncomfortable for a moment, then smiled and sighed, reaching back and dragging her bat forward and out of its holster. She rested it on her shoulders, letting her arms hang over the opposite ends of it like a scarecrow.

Mason asked, "Did we just level up?"

Ashley turned, the bat still up on her shoulders, and for a moment she looked as though she was going to say something sarcastic but then just burst out laughing. Mason and Donathan crowded in closer, echoing her laughter.

"Well! This is spectacular!" Nyla beamed, walking out of the crowd and motioning to their new outfits. "We should probably stay the night. It's safer, and we can get a good meal and refit the vehicle tomorrow morning."

Donathan, Ashley, and Mason all nodded excitedly as the coils overhead powered up with a hum, sending tendrils of blue and azure trickling down the fence line.

20.

Half Moon Bay

Zombie Civil Rights Group

Present Day

THE ENIAC QUIETLY DRIFTED over the bridge leading from Highway 101 into Half Moon Bay. Insects darted across a blue pond that spread out from under the bridge. The road trailed through the lush mountains. Green dominated the landscape here. Sagebrush with yellow-and-lime-tinted wild grass grew up to the edge of the road's shoulder. Cypress trees twisted in soft angles toward the sky with their bark peeled back in places, revealing white patches of pulp and wood beneath. The smell of eucalyptus found its way into the vehicle's cabin as the trees trailed past, their branches crossing high overhead. Yellow dandelions shook gently in the breeze, their bright color growing together in sporadic patches on the hillside. Old rusted street signs hung at crooked angles as the road wound among the thick brush. As the Winnebago continued down the road, they would often pass abandoned houses, their paint worn and chipped away from years of exposure to air thick with salt. Most of the houses seemed cozy and relaxing, even if vacant for decades.

At one point, Mason mumbled, "The beat is very calm here."

Ashley just sniffed a response. Even she seemed to be feeling the effects of this place.

As they got closer to the beach, a few burnt houses appeared.

"Falling Sands did that." Nyla's voice sounded bothered and strangely out of character for her. "They burnt quite a few homes and the enclave itself. When we reach Highway 1, you'll be able to see the extent of their damage."

The road narrowed and rose up a hill before trailing back down into a small ravine, and passed a gas station on its left. The plastic signs had been busted out of it sometime before, but the large shiny red truck parked nearby looked new and well maintained. Donathan crossed the cabin to the window on the right side, placed an arm up above his head and leaned on the window frame, staring at the truck longingly as they passed.

The vehicle screeched to a halt at a t-bone intersection. They were all staring at the enclave before Nyla pointed it out. Sheet metal lined a rounded base and led up to wooden planks, the tops of which were burnt black cinders. Chain-link fences surrounded most of the enclave, but near one end, they had been ripped apart, letting some of the chain trail off unnaturally across the ground, showing how forceful the assault that had torn through here had been. A large pole was jutting out of the top of the enclave, having fallen over and leaned against the north wall of the inside of the building.

Nyla sighed, "It really was one of a kind. They were testing a similar system to the one I created when they were attacked. Unfortunately, most of the scientists were killed before it was even demonstrated. That enclave was a technological wonder. It's hard to tell from here, but it's so vast that it actually extends back past the town of Miramar." Nyla frowned and looked back toward the road before adding, "Now it's just gutted."

Nyla gripped the dark steering wheel and slowly rounded its circumference with one hand then let it slide back through her grasp as the vehicle angled itself left and drove away from the enclave. The road widened into four lanes here. A deep valley extended on the left side of the road, light-green and emerald fields blending into brown and orange patches of grass. Crops could be seen growing wild and intermingling sporadically with large fields of weeds. A light fog of slight overcast drifted lazily over the adjacent hilltops.

No one said anything further, but there was a tranquil mood about the cabin as they passed a cliff's edge on the right and an old white motel on the left with a flagpole and a dirt parking lot. Large white columns rose two stories on its front side, framing the doorway and giving it a regal look. Tattered curtains drifted about its open windows.

The Eniac turned right and lumbered through a parking lot over several worn potholes as the sound of tags shifting about filled the inside of the vehicle. The RV eased to a halt, the rumble of the engine powered down, and the occupants all rushed outside.

The dusty brown sand of the parking lot meshed with white sand as it extended down the hill. Large logs of driftwood littered the grounds.

Ashley drew a sudden breath and sprinted away from the group and toward the water's edge. Her figure grew tiny as she sprinted down past a small inlet of trapped ocean water on the left, weaved her way around the edge of a cliff, and vanished over a dune.

The others picked their path between the crags and the water, avoiding the masses of driftwood and occasionally stopping to pick up a mussel shell or point out the hollow husk of a dead crab. The sound of the crashing waves grew louder as they crested the sand dune and found Ashley standing barefoot, feet dug into the wet sand, her shoes dangling from her left hand, and her long dark hair dancing about in the ocean breeze as white-capped aquamarine waves impacted the shoreline before them.

After a moment, Ashley turned around, and with eyes full of wonder, she said in a dreamy voice, "In another life... I would have been a surfer."

Donathan's smile widened as Mason giggled.

Nyla shrugged off the serenity and trudged up the beach, placing the large crumbling sea cliff on her left. Her pace seemed a bit rushed, and her steps took on a strange sense of determination. Everyone else trotted behind until Donathan finally broke ahead and caught up to Nyla's shoulder. The beach had begun to narrow next to the large bulk of the cliff.

Nyla glanced over at Donathan, then asked in a dark tone, "What do you know about Falling Sands?"

Donathan missed a step and stumbled, glanced back over his shoulders at his friends, and finally looked hesitantly in Nyla's direction and replied, "The usual: all enclaves pay tribute to them, they control most of California, including the bridge in Benecia, which is one of the last few ways out, and the slave trade is alive and well thanks to them."

Nyla nodded and stepped over a piece of driftwood before continuing, "When the darkness fell upon the world, it was the science enclaves who took it upon themselves to save it. Communication had been cut off, but that didn't mean we had to stop using trade and science."

Nyla stopped and studied the cliff a second. "So anyways, enclaves were born. At first, it was just out of necessity. The best possible way to survive the undead was to band together in small groups at night, then come out and scavenge and trade during the day when the dead had dispersed. Once the walls were thick and tall enough and there were enough supplies, you rarely heard about the undead overtaking a town."

Nyla stopped again and studied the cliff's edge. Donathan noticed small caves inside the crumbling beach rock. After a moment, Nyla strode up the beach again and continued, "That didn't mean people weren't eaten, killed, or turned all the time. Most of the world's big cities had fallen by then, and the need for trade was constant, so of course, people had to travel between the enclaves, and nightfall tended to punish most of the stragglers."

Donathan agreed. "Yeah, we're pretty familiar with this."

Nyla half smiled in his direction, and a seagull cawed off in the distance. "Enclaves began specializing in something that gave them a tradable commodity with the rest of the world. Some traded in supplies: food, clothing, water, whatever they could grow or produce. Others specialized in security services, minerals, wood, electronics, or goods from the world before; the scavenger enclaves were a very big deal for a while. During this time, science enclaves had sprung up strictly to find a cure or stop the spread of the undead in the world."

Nyla stopped, drew a breath, and looked back at everyone else. "You need to know that the science enclaves were not really a business then. The scientists had no sinister plans. All they wanted was to save the world. At least not most of them." Ashley raised an eyebrow in a confused manner, then let her eyes trail from Mason toward Donathan.

Nyla turned and walked back along the beach as a wave crashed on their right. She spoke again without bothering to look over her shoulder. "Science enclaves would pay Hunters during this time to try and bring in living or..." She stopped and looked up into the air with a far-off look in her eyes as everyone caught up again. "Maybe living isn't the word. Anyways, to bring in not-completely-dead zombies for experimentation." She turned a bit toward the cliff and walked toward a cave in the cliff side. "Then almost overnight, Falling Sands appeared."

Nyla deviated from her path a moment to stop and turn over a half-broken abalone shell and stare at it for a second, studying its translucent colors, before finally flipping it back over, standing up, and stepping through the sand, her small feet leaving a trail of footprints as she finally ducked into the gray-rock cave.

The sound of the ocean was muffled there, and they all crowded into the cramped space, ducking to make sure they didn't brush their heads on the rock as they pushed further back into the cave. Nyla stopped in front of a pile of rocks edging out from the side of the wall and turned around to face everyone. "Falling Sands created the trade, selling zombies to the science enclaves, creating the first harvester enclaves, and all the while taking tariffs and a portion of the profits to add to their growing enclave. No one really saw them as malicious in the early days. All of the science enclaves thought they were providing a service that brought in more undead to experiment on and hopefully find a cure for whatever was going on."

Ashley reached up to rub the scar on her cheek, never looking away from Nyla's bright eyes as the story continued.

"Falling Sands' enclave grew to mammoth proportions, and the fat cats running it grew prosperous off of the end of the digital age. Their life was comfortable while the rest of the world either worked or suffered. Then they brought back slavery."

Donathan coughed uncomfortably and shifted his feet around on the dark sand.

Nyla whispered slowly, "No one saw that coming. The world was already dark enough. Falling Sands began enslaving the members of smaller enclaves that weren't doing trade with them and began using the people to mine more raw materials near them. Somehow, their life of comfort wasn't good enough, and they had to ruin more lives just so that they could be richer while the rest of the world hid away every night."

Mason kneeled down, set his mask on the sand, took off his backpack, and fished around in it, pulling out paint bottles.

Nyla glanced over at him. Her voice growing gravelly and painful, she said, "My dad was the head scientist for the Half Moon Bay science enclave back then. He didn't trust Falling Sands. He knew that because we were one of the few places in the world the undead didn't travel to unless forced, they would eventually see us as a threat. So he made sure to build a secret lab with some resources where he could hide his data away from the prying eyes of the new world's ivory tower."

Stepping back past the edge of the rocks, she motioned to the corner of the cave. Donathan stepped forward, but it was Ashley who first said, "I see it."

In the gray mass of the crumbling cliff rock, painted the same color, was a large steel hatch, angled out so that the door opened up and out at a forty-five-degree angle away from the wall. Nyla wiped off a small digital pad next to it and keyed in a code.

Each key pressed issued a tiny chirp. Nyla finished with the last digit, and a loud hiss issued forth from the door, sending steam and stale air into the cave. "The stone in the cliff is terrible for construction projects, of course. But it's perfect for hiding a cement-and-steel-walled reinforced laboratory underground." Nyla beamed. "And terribly easy to burrow into before laying the cement." She stepped back as the steel hatch swung forward.

"Be careful, please." Nyla motioned to the dark doorway as Mason hung his mask back up on his head and gathered up his paint bottles. Nyla pointed toward the bottom of the doorway and added, "It can be hard to find the ladder in the dark here."

Aside from the light of a small red LED just overhead, located under the hatch, the tiny shaft they were descending was pitch black. The ladder's rungs made a gentle *thunk thunk* as boots and shoes stepped on and off the rungs. The floor below suddenly lit up with fluorescent bulbs. After another minute, Mason finally stepped off the final rung and placed a foot on hard concrete, looking around. The tunnel was a cement archway that extended forward into darkness. The only lights were four long bulbs in adjacent corners of the room where the roof met the walls.

"This way," Nyla added in her spacey tone. As she walked toward the darkness, another pair of fluorescent bulbs lit up on opposite sides, and the two bulbs behind them flickered out and went dark. The sudden change in lighting caused Mason to jump before hurrying forward to catch up with everyone else. After a few more feet, Nyla's voice chimed in again. "It's always cold down here. Never wet. The only time the tunnel is wet is if you use the door during high tide." The pale white cement made hollow noises that echoed up the tunnel as they walked. Nyla cleared her throat and then spoke in hushed tones, "The day Falling Sands attacked was something of a nightmare. We had defenses, but we hadn't anticipated a real zombie attack. Not like that, anyways."

Ashley sounded a little confused when she said, "Wait...so who attacked, Falling Sands or zombies?"

It was Nyla's turn to sound shocked as she spun around and faced everyone in the tunnel. "Both! You didn't know?" She let the moment register before continuing. "I saw him that day, The Judge. He looked like that dead French novelist, Balzac, his chest wide and shoulders large as if he was trying to mask the fact he was quite obese. He wore a blue cloak." Nyla laughed nervously and turned around to continue walking up the tunnel. "Can you imagine? A royal blue cloak—like he was some conquering hero." Their steps made a plunking sound below them, and the lights of the tunnel faded out. Nyla sighed and added, "I thought I had fixed the motion-sensor lights. Please jump up and wave your arms."

When the lights engaged with a deep hum, Ashley gasped. The room, bathed in light, was a vast two-story laboratory that extended down and one hundred meters in every direction. Strange machines of silver and white filled the bottom floor below them. Everyone was standing on a steel-mesh walkway in front of the dark tunnel entrance with a stairway five feet to their left, extending down to the lower floor. The walkway ran around the entire room, framing it and occasionally housing a desk pressed haphazardly up against the rail, giving space to work and still look down to see the center of the room. Several small holding cells with clear doors were on the lower far corner of the room.

Mason sprinted ahead and down the stairs to get a closer look at all the different equipment scattered around the room. Ashley and Donathan descended the stairs after Nyla.

Nyla spoke again, letting her voice echo behind her, "They attacked with Poisoners first. I'd never seen anything like them: bulbous bodies of tumors, issuing forth large sickly-green plumes of smoke from every pore. Their poison gets into everything, and once you've inhaled enough of it, you're paralyzed. Half of the compound was useless in a minute's time."

Donathan sniffed the air a minute, then shuffled his feet on the concrete.

Nyla didn't seem to notice and continued speaking, "Of course, by that time our security forces had started firing on them. That's when they hit our walls with every sort of explosive ordinance you can imagine. Rockets and flame were everywhere. It felt worse than any earthquake I have ever felt. That strange compression of explosives that presses against your face... it's... disorienting." Nyla's last syllable faded from across the room. Mason was standing in front of a large round-domed, canvas-covered machine perched in the center of the room. Its size dwarfed everything else in the lab. Several hoses seemed to extend out from under the canvas and snake across the floor in various directions all around the room. Nyla spoke again from the far side of the room. "The second a hole had been ripped in the wall of the enclave, all manner of undead rushed through. Their attack was coordinated, and I've never seen them work together like that. We had made preparations in case zombies ever did decide to come to Half Moon Bay, but we were not ready for such an attack. Scientists simply couldn't anticipate hundreds of different hordes working together. We didn't have the foresight for such a thing."

Mason leaned forward and spread the front flap of the canvas to unveil a large steel door covered in gears and cogs. A metal handle was placed horizontally across it, and a small round glass window was in the center of the door. Cupping his hands over his eyes, he leaned forward to peer into it. Once he had enough of his face pressed up against the glass, the glare disappeared, and he was staring into an inky black darkness that seemed lifeless. Suddenly, the darkness blinked at him. Mason jumped up, hit his head on the doorframe, and fell back. Nyla was standing next to him, looking down nervously.

"What...? There was...! How did you...?" Mason's voice was panicked.

Nyla just shrugged down at him, then turned and pulled the canvas back over the doorframe. "Dad's idea of an insurance policy for the world." She paused a moment, then added, "Probably best to leave that alone right now." She stepped back, spun on a heel, and walked back to the far corner of the room where the stairs bottomed out. Mason got to his feet, dusted himself off, and hurried back to where everyone else was standing, facing a wall full of gray monitors. One lone computer terminal was perched on the desk below the expanse of monitors that were all mounted at differing angles, as if placed by a child. When the wall had run out of space for monitors overhead, the person who mounted them had simply continued placing them on the next wall so the entire corner was filled with closed-circuit security footage.

"My stronghold!" Nyla beamed as she pulled back the desk chair and sat in front of the computer, her fingers becoming a blur, and the old Unix-based OS commands flickering across the screen as she worked on her task. The monitors came to life, showing black-and-white angles of various spots in Half Moon Bay. A CPU fan kicked on and added a hum to accompany the clicking of keystrokes that filled the open lab.

Donathan slid down against a wall next to various equipment. Ashley shrugged, dragged her baseball bat over her shoulder, and sat down against the wall next to the corner nook desk, with monitors high above her head, and shut her eyes, letting her bat rest on her lap. Mason's mask clattered as he dropped it to the cement floor. He then fished around in his pockets for a moment, eventually producing a green crayon. Flopping forward, his ballistic vest and contents made a ruckus as he lay down and colored the cement floor below him.

Donathan jumped a few minutes later, rubbing the back of his neck and looking behind him at the various pieces of lab equipment. "I swear something just bit—"

Nyla's computer monitor sprang to life in a sudden rush of sound, and the image of a man with disheveled black curly hair hunched forward toward the camera with thick-framed glasses and speaking in a monotone voice, "...and the Peripeteia device is a one-use device, so use it...well. To my dear daughter Nyla, I hope the device is never activated, and if it is, there's only a small chance that things wi—" His voice cut off suddenly, and the tones echoed into the hollow expanse of the cavernous laboratory. Everyone had cocked their heads up in confusion to watch the recording, and since the sound had faded, they all turned their attentions back to relaxing.

"That's all I can ever unlock from the recording..." Nyla sighed slowly and then added, "I don't even know how to activate the device."

Donathan's curiosity was piqued, "So what does it do?"

Nyla's informative tone stirred up, and she said, "Well to be put simply, it—" Nyla's head turned to observe a monitor for a moment before she added, "Oh, good; Princess Jae is home."

Donathan, Ashley, and Mason all lunged to their feet and flashed sign language furiously. For a full minute, everyone was arguing and vying to be the person being paid attention to. Nyla's desk chair made a squeaking sound as she spun around to observe the three friends huddled around each other, angry-faced and signing with determined movements.

"She said Princess Jae, didn't she?" Ashley signed while snapping her wrists.

"Yes, yes, yes, I heard it." Mason added.

Donathan's smile had dropped, and he looked annoyed. "We *never* asked her if she knew her? We never did. Why did we not ask her?"

"That's your fault, you know. You're the leader." Ashley's lips were tight, and her eyebrow was furrowed as she stared at Donathan.

"What happens now?" Mason asked.

Donathan just shrugged.

Ashley signed back, "We need to go find her. Before she disappears again."

Mason signed, "Maybe we should Nyla where Happy Birthday."

Donathan and Ashley both lowered their hands a moment and gave Mason disturbed looks.

Realizing something was wrong, Mason corrected himself and signed, "Maybe we should ask Nyla where she lives."

Nyla shouldered her way into the circle and signed in slow, fluid motions, "She lives at the top of a cliff, across a dirt clearing, in an old abandoned white motel. We passed it on our way into town."

"You know sign too?" Ashley asked, dumbfounded. "How long have you known sign?"

Nyla nodded and said, "Well... since I was a little girl—"

Donathan was already walking toward the stairs. "Never mind. Small talk later. Let's go find the Princess."

"If you don't mind..." Nyla announced behind the departing three, "I'll open the door to the tunnel from here. Uhh, if you don't mind, I'll stay here for a few more minutes doing some maintenance and catch up with you at Jae's house."

21.

Half Moon Bay

Zombie Civil Rights Group

Present Day

THE AIR WAS COLD and thick with salt. Donathan led the way as they crossed the dirt-and-sand parking lot outside the white hotel. A lone floodlight was mounted halfway up one of the large columns that extended up to the second floor of the hotel and framed a grand balcony overhead. Bugs could be seen fluttering in the lamplight and causing shadows to distort and stretch across the parking lot. The crashing ocean waves were a dull hum. Donathan stopped suddenly, hunched his shoulders forward, and aimed one of his pistols at the hotel. Ashley took a step to his right and did the same with her rifle. Mason just stepped to the left and then peered forward, letting his machine gun dangle off his weapon sling.

"I don't care what Nyla says about Half Moon Bay," Ashley whispered. "It's still creepy walking around at night."

Donathan lowered his pistol slowly. "I don't really see any movement."

Mason joined in the whispering. "Isn't she supposed to be our friend or...?"

Donathan looked back at him out of the corner of his eye and said, "I don't know what she is, honestly. Just that Dad said *find* her."

Ashley started to whisper and then choked out a noise before taking a deep breath and asking, "We don't know why we're looking for her? ALL this TIME and we don't know WHY we're looking for her?" Her whisper had somehow taken on a shrill tone.

Donathan just shrugged and walked up to the hotel's front door, then slowly pushed it open with little force. The door's semi-rusted hinges gave a small squeak as they eased the wooden door back. "It's open," he added before disappearing inside. Ashley and Mason rushed after him and stepped into the hotel's main foyer.

Once-light-yellow wallpaper hung loose off the walls everywhere. Large holes were ripped in all of the walls, leaving broken drywall scattered across the floor, lining the walls in some places. An old lead-lined steel refrigerator with a round door was perched against the far left wall, standing on stubby four-inch legs. Much of its tan paint had chipped off and showed the plain steel finish shining through. On the far side of the room, a small doorway could be seen behind a concierge desk that was partially collapsed. A staircase lined the right wall, with dusty wooden pin-top balusters leading up to an oak handrail that went straight up to a landing on the second floor, where a large canvas fire-hose was wound into a glass cubby labeled, In Case of Fire. High above the center of the room was a large chandelier with two working bulbs casting a light glow in the room. Just under that was a rusted metal car axle dangling precariously below the chandelier with two thick ropes. Smaller ropes lined the ceiling above it, trailing out to all corners of the room in a strange crisscross pattern.

Ashley sighed and looked at Mason, asking, "Is this your doing?"

Mason looked up around the roof, letting his eyes follow the trails of the rope webbing. "No," Mason said firmly. "I uhh..." Mason's voice took on a confused tone. "No, I didn't—"

The room buzzed with the sound of feedback a second before an old piano chimed in, playing a slow, melodious tune. Determined notes drifted around the room when the lights flickered off and purple black-lights lit up, hung hidden in the webbing just overhead. The glowing effect of the webbing on the rest of the room was disorienting. Colors that had previously been invisible appeared, splattered randomly all over the room.

"Over there." Donathan pointed across the room to a painting that had appeared near the refrigerator. The painting's colors didn't contrast at all. The green hair, purple skin, and yellow camisole t-shirt seemed jarring, but the creepiest parts of the painting were the big red splotches for eyes that seemed to be staring up at the ceiling.

"What an ugly painting," Donathan commented with disgust before looking over at Mason.

"Don't look at me," Mason said, shocked. "It looks like impressionism threw up a circus clown. I wouldn't do that—"

Ashley interrupted, saying, "Go over there," and motioning toward the painting.

Donathan took one step before the piano music's volume went up a notch and he froze in place.

"Okay... Mason, you go over there." Ashley was practically yelling over the dark tones of the piano music, but she still managed to sound nervous.

"Hell no!" Mason shouted. "Every single one of my nightmares begins like this."

Frustrated, Ashley finally shouted, "Okay, fine!" She strolled across the room toward the painting, "You two babies want to be scared by some music and some blacklights, fine. Be babies." She stood directly in front of the painting, then turned around to face Mason and Donathan across the room before shouting, "See! It's just a fucking painting! She's just trying to scare us!"

The painting stirred.

Donathan's smile faded, and Mason's mouth dropped.

"WHAT?" Ashley shouted in frustration. The painting lurched out of its frame, wrapping its arms around a screaming Ashley, and dragged her through it into darkness before a wooden plank slapped down, covering it from the other side. Ashley's ear-piercing scream tore through the room as Donathan surged forward to the painting and Mason ran over. By the time Mason got there, Donathan was already smashing his shoulder into the wooden board repeatedly, causing the floor to shake with each wooden thump. Mason rubbed his temple with one hand and turned back around toward the center of the room as Donathan continued to slam his shoulder into the blockade over and over.

"If I could just get enough—" *Whump.* Donathan smashed his shoulder into the board, then leaned back to see if it had given any more.

Mason's eyes focused on the car axle hanging in the center of the room as one of the ropes popped free. Half of the car axle swung down, causing the rest of it to bounce and sway as it hung from a single rope off the chandelier.

Thump! Whump! Donathan slammed his shoulder into the wooden board two more times in succession, and the car axle shook again, its weight throwing itself around with a strange volatile presence, since it was hanging vertically.

"Hey, maybe we shouldn't be—" Mason's voice was confused as his eyes trailed from the car axle and back to Donathan, who was still focused on the wooden board.

Wham! Donathan slammed his shoulder back into the board again.

"Donathan. Please stop—" Dread was overflowing in Mason's voice as he watched the car axle twitch once more.

Whump! Donathan backed up two steps and snapped forward a kick, the heel of his boot colliding hard against the wooden board.

All at once, the last rope holding the car axle overhead snapped off, and the sound of rope straining could be heard as the axle fell a foot then suddenly rotated back horizontally due to smaller ropes lashed across each end. The webbing of the ceiling fell forward a moment, then tensed and stretched, revealing the mass was held aloft by hundreds of other smaller woven ropes.

"I think I heard the board give a little," Donathan said as Mason squeaked, his face contorted into a sour look of fear, his eyes about as wide as they could be. He took one last look in Donathan's direction and reached up, grasping the edge of his mask tensely and lowering it swiftly to reveal a picture of Mason, his face contorted into a sour look of fear, his eyes about as wide as they could be painted in acrylics over the hockey mask.

Finally noticing Mason's fear, Donathan spun around just in time to see the car axle arc down and forward, smashing both of them into the hotel wall.

The crowd murmured among themselves as they pushed forward. Standing across the street in the morning sun with a frustrated look on her face was Ashley. Dark hair flowed back into a woven ponytail over the brown shoulders of a Star Wars Jedi robe, and in her right hand was a replica lightsaber, powered off. "Hurry up, for Christ's sake. It's already almost noon."

Ashley turned to rush up the small steps of San Francisco's Moscone Center, passing a group of excited superheroes on her left and some Mortal Kombat cosplayers smoking menthol cigarettes on her right. The building had a grand amount of glass and a minimalist amount of steel, the second floor overhanging the lower entrance where the doors were. Ashley went to follow the crowd through the center glass doors and quickly realized something, turning around to shout out, "Mason, you have my ticket!"

A mad hatter stepped up and removed his purple top hat and fished furiously inside his green vest. After a moment, he kneeled down and produced items from his pockets and placed them on the pavement while mumbling to himself. The assortment of things on the cement in front of him became a pencil, a pen, a pad of paper, three candy cigarettes, an empty Tic Tacs box, a phone charger, and an ancient television remote control. After a moment, he reached back into his vest, produced three crumpled pieces of printer paper, and unfurled and straightened one out before handing it to Ashley.

Donathan walked up in jeans and a black trench coat, taking a second sheet out of Mason's hand. Mason gathered up his items, shoving them back into his pockets.

Ashley turned to Donathan, rolled her eyes, and added, "Could you at least try to get into the spirit?" She turned and handed the paper to the attendant and stepped through the glass doorway.

Donathan called out behind her, "I'm Butcher... from Garth Ennis's *The Boys*." He looked down at his arms and then back up, asking, "What's wrong with my costume?"

Inside, the trio passed Ryu and Ken from Capcom's *Street Fighter* and pushed through people until they were all standing shoulder-to-shoulder, facing the front door with a banner directly above it reading WonderCon.

The air was abuzz with conversation and cell phone camera shutter noises as people in costumes occasionally stopped to line up next to each other. A Psylocke excused herself as she pushed between Donathan and Ashley for the doorway ahead.

"I've waited all year for this... and we're late." Ashley didn't even try to hide the contempt in her tone.

"It's not that big of a deal," Mason replied. "After all, there's still tomorrow."

"Tomorrow's tide breaks at 7:00 a.m. That's still more important." Excitement crept into Ashley's voice, "OHMYGOD! Did you see that Darth Maul costume?" Maniacal laughter crept in as she said, "So many costumes to see..."

"I think the food court serves beer," Donathan observed.

Ashley sighed.

Mason chimed in, "At 2:00 p.m., the creators of *The Walking Dead* are speaking!"

Ashley looked over her left shoulder toward Mason and said in a monotone, "Zombies... really...?"

Mason drew a breath and then quietly added, "Darkness is my litany. Every night I pretend I creep alongside the undead, trying to avoid detection and praying for a sidearm... and every day, light is my savior and my curse as I step lightly to avoid other survivors."

Two people dressed as Vulcans had stopped midstep to tilt their heads in Mason's direction, straining to hear the words rolling off his tongue.

"I definitely need a drink," Donathan remarked, disappearing into the crowd toward the food court.

Ashley had already disappeared into the main foyer ahead. After a moment, Mason followed her path into the chaos ahead of him.

Excited shouts rose up inside the main hall. Mason was suddenly surrounded by vendors and fans rushing off to different places to meet actors or pursue that difficult-to-find final issue of *The Flaming Carrot*. Girls dressed as anime characters Mason didn't recognize drifted past, whispering about how Felicia Day really is that tiny in person.

Mason drifted toward the nearest booth with cardboard boxes of comics and action figures mounted on its plastic mesh walls alongside various marker-written price tags. For a moment, the crowd faded around him, and he was lost in the font of the price tags alongside their wares, admiring the curve and gentle grace of the scribbled numbers.

"You have a good eye," the blond girl dressed up as a female version of Mario next to him added. "That's a rather hard to find issue of *TMNT*. I love the blood and gore of the original series."

Mason turned suddenly in her direction and managed to drop his hat and lose the remote control from his pocket. Scrambling to fix this situation, he looked back up, meeting the gaze of her baby-blue eyes and added, "I don't...what?"

"That issue. Raphael gets sucked into a weird time dimension on the freeway where people speed in this surreal world of M.C. Escher-esque landscapes and..." The blue eyes finally caught up with his stunned stare. "Hi...I'm Elaine."

Her smile could melt kryptonite, Mason thought. "I'm...I mean. What?"

Elaine giggled a moment. "How about we start with the basics?" She reached out her hand and took Mason's right hand in hers. "And you are?"

"Uhh, Mason," he managed to croak.

An amused Elaine nodded appreciatively. "And, Mason, what do you do?"

"Well, for a living... I'm, uh..." Mason stammered out, "I'm a mathematician."

A scream erupted from the peaceful chaos of the crowd at the convention. The shriek carried an unusual depth to it, as if the universe itself was caving in around it. The volume and tone of fear held in the air could have been maintained by an opera singer. Only Mason seemed to notice the high-pitched wail and dropped his gaze to look around the large hall, his eyes searching for the source of such frustration.

"A mathematician?" Elaine asked, her curious eyes still resting on Mason's face. "And what do you do for fun?"

Mason finally stopped wondering about the voice and turned back toward her to answer, "I mostly go to furry conventions—"

The world ripped and tore as Mason awoke, frantically twisting and thrashing about. The scream rose to an apex of wailing crossed with a mishmash of hoarse yowling and tears.

22.

Half Moon Bay

Zombie Civil Rights Group

Present Day

FIVE MINUTES LATER, Mason was still screaming.

"Shut *up*! Shut the *hell* up!" Ashley's voice was shrill but sounded almost musical in her frustration. "God damn your furry nightmares. I wish you'd wake up screaming about zombies just once."

Mason continued blubbering and whimpering for a minute before he tried to get up and came to a cold realization. "My arms are tied behind my back."

Ashley replied quietly, "Yeah, no shit. After she yanked me through that hole in the wall and stungunned me, she dragged me upstairs and tied me up. She brought the rest of you up later... D is still passed out. All

I can see of the room is a window and a door..." Ashley's words trailed off as she noticed the woman with dark, judging eyes standing in the doorway.

Mason said, "I don't really see anything but a wall here. I can wiggle around, though—" A *whump* echoed in the room, followed by the clatter of a plastic mask as Mason fell over and squirmed and kicked his feet awkwardly.

"Mason, stop," Ashley whispered in a cautious voice.

The woman in the doorway was tall and had long brown hair that draped down past her shoulders and thin eyebrows that arched just under a set of bangs. She wore a black San Francisco Giants zip-up sweater that seemed relatively clean and a pair of jeans whose legs were thick and baggy. A small amount of the blacklight-reactive paint could still be seen on her cheeks and forehead. She let her sinister stare drop a moment as she broke the line of sight by raising an old 1920s cloche hat and pulling it down tight on her head. The white hat and black ribbon across it contrasted well with the black and orange sweater with white print.

Mason was still kicking and making grunting noises on his side, trying to get a view of the rest of the room. He had succeeded in wiggling about forty-five degrees around when the woman walked through the room, grabbed him forcefully by the back of his ballistic vest, and yanked him up and around so he was propped next to Ashley. Donathan was still passed out up against the wall behind the two.

Mason whispered out the side of his mouth, "Why didn't you tell me—"

The woman cleared her throat and then reached into her jeans pocket, producing an old Ziploc bag. A slight shuffling sound of plastic could be heard as she opened it and searched through it. After a moment, she drew out a tiny book made of fabric. Kneeling down directly in front of the trio she opened it up, revealing sewing needles with red, purple, and green stains across the tips of them. She looked up and gave a long sinister stare toward Mason, then her eyes seemed to glaze over in thought.

After an uncomfortable minute, Mason finally tried to start a conversation. "So, uh—" In an instant the women ripped out one of the sewing needles and jammed it into Mason's shoulder.

"Ahhh! Ahhhh! Ahhh! Ahhhh! She stabbed me! She stabbed me, Ash! Ahhhh—"

The woman's stern voice echoed over Mason's screams. "You know, most of the world has forgotten the old weapons." She stood up, still holding the fabric book in one hand but continuing to stare at Mason as if studying him. Mason's screams tapered off, and the woman continued, "It's a shame really. Some of the old weapons were nasty."

"What did you do?" Ashley's voice was quiet, cold and defensive. It carried with it the tone of a snake that seemed coiled and ready to strike.

The woman replied without care, continuing her monologue, "Flesh-eating bacteria, for instance. Now, that makes a good weapon."

"I've got flesh-eating bacteria in me?" Mason screeched as he fell over again, struggling.

"Or it could be anthrax. Do you feel feverish and chilly at the same time?" She asked, looking down on Mason.

"Oh my god...eeh...mehhhh..." Mason's struggling grew weak. "Ash, I feel... I'm sweaty."

Ashley said in a sympathetic voice, "Mason. It'll...It's gonna be okay." Then she looked up with accusing eyes at the woman and asked, "Why would you do this?"

Princess Jae smiled in an amused manner, refolded and tucked the fabric book back into the Ziploc pouch, then dropped it on the floor, asking, "Who sent you?" Acid seemed to drip off the syllables.

Mason had begun wheezing. "We don't... I mean... Just... Well, it's not even really my choice—"

"Your friend doesn't look too good," Jae interrupted.

Ashley's confused and nervous train of thought turned into anger. "Look, we have been looking for a goddamned five years now, and it's not like it's exactly been easy—"

"You know," Jae's voice sounded strained as she reached into her pocket again, "I've got quite a few other concoctions here—"

"My last name is Wilkens!" Donathan shouted over Ashley's shoulder, causing her to flinch in surprise. Thirty seconds of uncomfortable silence passed, aside from Mason's gasping from where he was lying. Donathan took a deep breath and added, "She's Ashley Plum, and that's—"

"The Meeks boy, Mason." Jae finished his sentence and rushed forward, untying Mason.

Ashley's voice was shrill and frustrated. "Yeah, the one you *poisoned*!"

Princess Jae let the accusation stand as she finished untying Mason and dragged him back up to a sitting position, then scrambled for his mask, perching it on the top of his sweaty forehead. "He's not poisoned." Her voice was dry and a little amused. She untied Ashley. "Those were sewing needles marked with crayons I found in an abandoned art supply store."

All of the color rushed back to Mason's face, and in one fluid motion he leapt to his feet, yelling, "Art supply store?"

After everyone was untied, Donathan filled in Jae about his dad's final words on finding the other children of friends and her; about his enclave being overrun by the Protectorate when he was young; about his parents always having spoken highly of Jae; about how he'd managed to hide under their noses for so many years, escape, and then track and find Ashley and Mason; and about how they'd almost made a game of surviving the darkness ever since then. He even went over the running joke of calling themselves the Zombie Civil Rights group. The only time the conversation lulled was when Princess Jae walked them out of the room to the landing to lead them back to their weapons, bags, and mp3 players.

"Look, I loved your families too, but I just don't understand why he sent you. The Protectorate and most of the Shytown Trail hates me just as much as they hate you... and you're grown now and have figured out how to survive. What are we supposed to do here? The world has already gone to hell five times over. Did none of you ever stop to think maybe I'm not your answer?"

All three of them just stared at her, blank-faced.

The silence ended with Mason asking, "What about this art supply store?"

Ashley drew a breath and then stopped a moment because she heard a popping noise in the distance.

Jae sprinted over to the window and edged out, peering cautiously through it. With another pop, purple light flooded into the room. Princess Jae spun around, almost losing her hat in the process. In a short burst of rage, she shouted at Ashley, Mason, and Donathan, "You led them here?"

She sprinted back across the room toward the far wall while letting a stream of frustration echo in the room. "All these years, I've managed to avoid them here, and you put them on my front doorstep. Of course, you're damn fools." Her hands drifted over the wall, searching for something. "You're all just kids who were never allowed to be kids. I can't believe..." Part of the wall moved back, and she slid through it, vanishing out of sight.

Donathan was already on the wall trying to figure out where it opened.

Ashley sprinted to the window with Mason right behind her. In the sky above them, fireworks popped and hissed, leaving purple star clusters drifting slowly. As they leaned out the window, using the flashes of light for illumination, they could see two Protectorate army soldiers below with their masks and rifles, sprinting across a field of...

"Artichokes!" Ashley moaned.

She was shouting at them before Mason knew what was going on. "Hey, you! Right there!" The soldiers stopped and turned their dark masks toward Ashley, who was hanging out of the second floor window of the motel. "Yeah, you! You're here for us, right?"

The dumbfounded soldiers looked at each other and then back to Ashley, nodding slowly.

"That's fine. We'll be down in five minutes, but *get off the damn artichokes!*" She motioned for them to move toward a path. "We have no issues with you coming for us, but just for the love of God, stop trampling the artichokes already."

The soldiers stepped over to the path as she continued her rant. Just before her last word, another soldier tried to go running past across the artichokes, but one of the others held up his hands to stop him and motion him over to the path. All three of them stood there a moment and then looked up at Ashley in the window.

"Five minutes. We'll be right down."

Climbing back out of the window's frame, Ashley pushed past Mason toward Donathan, who had given up on trying to open the wall. "Better get your Puppy Suits ready; those guys are dumb as hell. We might have three minutes until they realize it and come in after us. What do we do?"

Donathan's smile had faded for once. "I don't...I didn't think she'd ditch us. It's not exactly what I expect—"

Ashley took her tiny hands and grabbed the collar of his trench coat, looked up at him, and said in a determined tone, "You're our goddamned glue and our leader. Just get us out of this."

Donathan seemed to find control and asked, "What about her weird trap?"

Ashley shook her head. "No. I'm pretty sure I heard her cut it down and roll it across the room to get to you guys."

"How much ammo do you guys have?" Donathan was already dropping the magazine of one of his pistols to check rounds.

Mason quietly replied, "A belt."

Unhappy with what she saw when she cleared her rifle, Ashley chucked it across the room and drew her bat.

Mason's eyes were wide. He was standing five feet back and staring out the window as if he'd finally realized what was happening. Donathan crossed the room and walked out the door to the front stairway landing. A *thunk* sounded, followed by a crescendo of shattered glass. Ashley followed, and Mason rushed out of the room behind her. They were greeted by Donathan holding a fire hose, his smile returning to his cheeks. "I guess we pray Nyla kept the water pressure going in the town all these years. Suddenly realizing what he planned, Ashley sheathed her bat, took the fire hose from Donathan, spun around and stuck the copper nozzle in Mason's hand. Mason looked down at the nozzle, letting his eyes follow the massive trail of hose from his hand across seven feet of floor and back into its hutch, where it was coiled and folded neatly.

Mason looked back up at his friends and said, "I'm confused."

Donathan's smile widened over Ashley's shoulder. Ash gave Mason a wicked smile and said, "Make art."

Looking down at the hose, then back at his friends and then down the stairs and around the room, Mason puffed out an excited breath.

Loud *clop-clop* noises rang out as two men in dark, shiny uniforms sprinted into the hotel's front entrance, both wearing masks with breathing apparatuses and holding rifles. They both froze and turned their ominous triangular eyes toward the second floor landing when Ashley said, "Hey guys, welcome to the party!" A loud whistling noise preceded the spray of water rushing through ancient pipes as Donathan spun the wheel, opening the valve to the fire hose. At first, the soldiers just stared in wonder. Then the first baluster snapped, causing a loud crack. The hose's long form had been wound in a trail down through the stairs and balusters and across the handrail. Wood broke and ripped, sending splinters showering throughout the room. The hose twitched and inflated violently at the end of the stairs, then its mass darted across the room, where it was lassoed around the old metal refrigerator.

After a moment, the fridge fell over, and more of the hose's bulk filled up, this time crisscrossing back across the room and up toward the chandelier. It broke free of the ceiling with a snap and the tinkling of prisms then came crashing down on the soldiers in a loud collision of broken glass, steel, and flooring.

Mason stood up slowly from the platform above, shouldering his machine gun and said, "I call this piece... oh, shit."

The hose continued filling, and its length snaked back into the plaster holes in the wall of the house. The wall burst instantly, sending plaster shattering across the room and ripping a trail back up toward the three friends. Donathan frantically tried to shut the valve off, only to come away holding the metal wheel in his hand, staring at it wide-eyed.

After a moment, the hose ripped free and spasmodically flung itself back downstairs.

Ashley looked around at all the damage and the spraying water, then turned toward Mason and said, "You almost outdid yourself this t—"

The entire motel collapsed around them.

23.

Half Moon Bay

Zombie Civil Rights Group

Present Day

"MAAASOOON. AAASHLEEEY. Maaasooon."

Mason sat up, shaking his head. The smell of dust and sand filled the air. After another moment, he realized that voice was real.

"I'm here!" Mason shouted back. "I'm on...in...? I'm somewhere in the house. It's pretty dark here."

Donathan's reply sounded relieved. "Okay, stay there, but try to keep shouting. I think I know where you are."

Mason shouted about how amazed he was that he brought the house down and how if he ever got a second chance to do it, he'd try to get the hose up through the ceiling first because that might have created a much cooler effect of broken boards raining down through the house. Finally, he heard the sound of a wooden board shifting directly overhead, and sunlight poked through. Mason stood up and poked his upper torso through the rubble before taking a moment to admire his work.

The whole side and back of the house had collapsed. The stairs had vanished, replaced with piles of broken boards, their long splintered and shattered masses twisted up with the ripped and tattered carpet that had once wrapped up them. Most of the second floor landing had collapsed, and what few parts of it still remained connected had slanted and warped almost vertically down. The floorboards from the landing had wrenched and scattered across the room as part of the roofing had caved in above it, sending tiles cascading in and across the pile of chaos. Somehow his creation had upheaved part of the floor, adding a large wave of boards in the middle, and through the dust still hanging in the air, he could see dark blue sky and stars beginning to fade. "The sun must be coming up," Mason added, sounding lost.

Boards shifted near the back of the room, and the coughing form of Ashley stood up, dusting herself off and sending some of the planks clattering down around her. When the coughing faded and she finally seemed satisfied with the dust, she accepted the hand of Donathan, who had rushed over and climbed up above the mess. Mason joined them after a moment of shifting over the debris. The trio spent a moment reacquiring their weapons and shouldering their backpacks before making their way through refuse toward the front of the motel.

The door to the motel was still standing somehow, and when they finally managed to climb over to it, Donathan realized the frame had tapered and warped from all the shifting of the building, so the door had been wedged shut. Dust rained down as Donathan finally managed to heel-kick the door open while sitting awkwardly on the pile of junk. All three of them slid down through the door... and into hell.

Waves crashed in the distance, and although the sun hadn't peeked up yet, the dark blue sky was definitely beginning to light up over Half Moon Bay. A large throng of soldiers extended out from the rubble on each side of the house, their lines tapering out near the cliff edge, a dune behind one of the groups. Their forms were lined up orderly, shoulder-to-shoulder, shiny black armor to shiny black armor, the copper-metalwork-lined masks all turned toward the three members of the Zombie Civil Rights group. In the middle of the clearing in her white and blue armor, with the cliff to her back, sword handle peeking out above one shoulder, stood Mary Helen, sneering wickedly.

"Don't be shy," Mary Helen's voice boomed. "It's not like you've anywhere to go. Your running days are over." The lines of soldiers erupted in deep laughter as if their general had belted out some amazing one-liner on stage at some long-forgotten comedy club.

Mary Helen's smile dropped, and she raised a hand to silence her men. Donathan stepped forward, away from the house and into the clearing. Mason and Ashley stepped up a second later and stood alongside him, glaring out at the General of the Protectorate Army.

Taking the cue, Mary Helen turned to one side and paced while shaking her head. "Knocking over enclaves on our trail, disrupting our trade and income, but perhaps your biggest mistake was just being a general nuisance for me." Her pacing stopped, and she turned to face the trio, her head tilted downward, her eyebrows furled. The tiny one donned an evil stare before she added, "I am tired of chasing you up and down this goddamned state."

Donathan stepped forward and planted a determined foot down, and every soldier surrounding them raised a rifle in one fluid motion.

"Ohh, I wouldn't." Mary's voice seemed to goad Donathan to take another step. "I wouldn't try my little speed-magic trick. As fast as you are, I'm pretty sure a battalion of bullets all directed at you and your friends might just trump you." Donathan stepped back and stood in place.

Mary Helen looked amused. "Yeah, I read your file, and it's not like you don't have a history with the Protectorate, Donathan Wilkens." Ashley shot a confused look at Mason, who shrugged back at her.

"So here's what's going to happen." Mary Helen's voice had some elation to it. "I'm going to take on each of you... one at a time. Just for the amusement of my soldiers." Laughter rose up throughout the crowd. "If you run, they'll open fire. Trust me when I tell you I'll live and you won't. When I've finally had my fun..." Her tiny form stepped forward, and she jammed a thumb to her chest in a childlike way. "When I've had my fill of beating you down... I am going to kill one of you. Then I'm going to disfigure one of you... the pretty one, perhaps?"

Donathan held up a hand to his face and added quietly, "Aw, man." Ashley raised an eyebrow in curiosity and shock and slowly turned her head to stare at Donathan a moment.

Mary Helen continued, "Then the two survivors are going to work the rest of their lives as slaves in the mines just outside of Falling Sands." Mary Helen cleared her throat, then added, "But it won't be all bad. I'll make sure the work you get is hard and dangerous enough that you won't live long enough to really suffer." She donned another sinister smile as the last word faded, and more laughter rose up around them all.

Mary Helen stretched, tilting her neck from one side to the other and then drew her right foot back, held up her hands in a fighting stance, and said, "Right, support by fire goes first."

Mason, Donathan, and Ashley just stood there as a minute passed. Finally, Ashley whispered, "She means you, Mason."

"Oh," Mason replied as he took two steps forward, then asked confusedly over his shoulder, "What uhh... what do I do?"

"She wants you to fight her," Donathan said.

"Oh," Mason added once more and then reached for his machine gun, shouldered at his side, only to find that when he had strapped it back on in the dark and broken husk of the house, he had put it on backward so the muzzle pointed behind him and the butt of the gun was pointed out. Instead of reslinging it, Mason just slowly turned around and tried to line up the barrel with Mary Helen while looking sheepishly over his right shoulder. The safety clicked off on hundreds of rifles around them.

"No no no no no no...NO," Ashley interjected. "She means without weapons." Mary Helen had lowered her fists and stood up straight, sighing audibly at this point.

"Oh," Mason echoed again before unslinging and setting down his machine gun in the sand of the parking lot. He also drew off his backpack, set it down in the sand, unzipped it, and began fumbling through it for something. The clinking of plastic and glass paint bottles echoed from the pack. Mason straightened his mask from its spot on the top of his head and finally stood up, holding a small bottle with a spray-bottle nozzle in each of his hands. Mary Helen drew her stance back and brought her fists up as Mason walked cautiously forward.

When he was just a few feet away from her, Mason held out his right hand and presented the bottle of perfume to Mary Helen, who flinched. Mason stopped dead in his tracks and then said, "No. It's okay. Smell this."

Confusion streaked across Mary Helen's face as she dropped her stance and stood back up. Finally she leaned out past Mason and locked eyes on Donathan and Ashley while asking, "Is he serious?"

Ashley answered dryly as she shrugged, "Probably. We don't...who knows?"

"Just smell it. It's safe, I promise." Mason was still holding his arm up but edged a bit closer.

Still confused, Mary Helen locked her frustrated gaze on Mason, leaned forward, and smelled the lilac scent of perfume from the bottle Mason was holding. For a moment, she forgot the dust, the undead, the army, and even the mission as the scent overwhelmed her and she was taken back to a simpler time, when the world wasn't so cutthroat. She leaned back, not quite sure what to say or how to respond, then felt something brush her armor near her hip. Looking down, she saw Mason's other hand furiously pumping sprays of perfume onto Mary Helen's backside. She jumped back, ran her hand down over the wet armor and held it up to her nose to smell what it was. This time, rose-scented perfume filled her lungs, but she was far less enthusiastic about the scent. She dropped her hand and asked, "What the *fuck*? You sprayed my ass with *perfume*?" Her mouth was open with shock, and her head was cocked forward.

Mason's eyes were wide, and he wore the look of a child who had just been caught stealing candy. Slowly, his right hand raised up, and when it got just past his chest, it darted forward toward Mary Helen and sprayed perfume into her mouth.

Mary Helen coughed and sputtered, then in one quick motion roundhouse-kicked Mason and sent him skidding off to the side of the clearing where he came to rest in a crumpled heap of flesh. He didn't move as the dust settled around him and laughter echoed up from the soldiers surrounding them all. Mary Helen was hunched forward, spitting and ranting out syllables of curse words.

Ashley looked over at Mason's body. His mask was face down next to his feet, having toppled off after the kick. She couldn't see his face from where she was standing, just an arm and his legs flailed out unnaturally while he was face down in the sand.

"I've had about enough of this bitch." Ashley was already stepping forward and drawing the bat out over her shoulder.

Mary Helen stood back up, drew one leg back and unsheathed the sword over her shoulder. "Finally"—her tone became dark as she angled the sword over her head, pointing the tip toward Ashley's form—"a real fight."

Ashley drew her foot back and gripped the base of the bat with both hands, looking down her shoulder at Mary Helen as if waiting for her to pitch a baseball.

The tide rose and fell as the two girls just stared at each other waiting for one to make a move.

Finally, Ashley screamed and sprinted forward, her feet trampling the sand as she rushed ahead, *piff piff*. Once she closed the gap, Ashley brought her shoulder around and let the bat carry forward in two hands to meet the sword. Sparks showered around them as aluminum and steel collided in the dark morning hour. Letting the weight carry the swing through, Ashley dropped one hand and let her other follow back around as the one hand swung the bat up to strike Mary Helen, who was already shifting the sword back down to counter. Again the clang from metal on metal sounded.

Mary Helen swung forward and tried to let the sword carry itself down the mass of the bat toward Ashley's hands.

Ashley promptly swung the bat up and around the sword, stepped back, and spun a kick toward Mary Helen, who stepped back and let the kick miss and then took the opportunity to arc her sword toward Ashley's shoulder, but she had already let her body spin out, down, and away, flourishing her bat behind her as she went.

Ashley spun and flicked her bat once as she stood up, as if she was flinging blood off an old katana. Ash brought the bat back into both hands then swung forward, letting go and sending the bat flying toward her opponent. Ashley sprinted behind the flung bat, hoping to bring a foot or a fist down behind it.

With ease, Mary Helen sprinted forward, brought her legs up, and spun up and over the side-flung bat. As her body came tumbling down, she brought her sword hilt forward and down ahead of her onto the top of Ashley's head. Ashley's body collided with the packed sand with a *whump*. When Mary Helen stepped away and the dust cleared, Ashley was face down, one of her legs twitching unconsciously in the sand.

"Two down," Mary Helen added as the soldiers erupted with laughter. "A gunslinger left." Surprise crossed Mary Helen's face, and she added in sudden realization,

"The gunslinger... you want to shoot me, don't you?"

Donathan's eyes were still darting from Ashley's twitching body back to Mason's.

Mary Helen continued, "You want to shoot me? That's your big thing, running around and firing pistols, isn't it? You couldn't even scratch me if you wanted to."

Donathan still hadn't looked up.

Mary Helen's rant continued, "You want to"—sarcasm entered her voice—"gun me down in cold blood at high noon?" Some of the soldiers' laughter surrounding them became huge belly laughs at this point. "You can't... Bullets can't even hurt me. Go on, cowboy... bet you that you can't even hu—" Three shots collided with Mary Helen's upper torso, and she jolted back, sliding across the ground a few feet before coming to rest in the dust and sand, face up to the sky, then light blue.

Donathan held a smoking gun and asked out loud, "Why does everyone think I'm a gambler? Is it the trench coat?"

Ashley stirred and then stood up, rubbing her head. She looked from Mary Helen back to Donathan and the soldiers, none of whom were laughing but all of whom were staring down their iron sights at them. Figuring she didn't have much to lose, she jogged over toward Donathan.

Mary Helen gasped from the flat of her back and then sat up. "Just enough—" she coughed and hacked as she stood up. "I bet you're thinking, 'If only I had aimed better for her head,' but—"

In one fluid motion, Donathan shot her again in the head and sent her body falling in a backward arc into the dust again. He continued firing at her body as it collapsed until the pistol made a metallic click.

Donathan sighed and said to Ashley, "I've got calluses on my trigger finger, you know... but the damn thing is still itchy."

Ashley laughed nervously, motioning to all the soldiers around them.

Mary Helen flexed backward where she was lying, kicked her legs up, and let the momentum carry her back up and forward onto her feet. She walked toward them without a scratch on her. "As I was saying before I was so rudely interrupted, I bet you thought shooting me in the head would have been the way to go... but as you can see"—she stopped and let one hand trail down from her head toward her legs—"you can't even bruise me."

Donathan unconsciously looked at his empty pistol and back up in confusion.

Mary Helen taunted them further, "You can't fucking touch me. I'm *goddamned* invincible."

Mason stood up suddenly, screaming about furries and shifting about frantically. Mary Helen turned to face him as he calmed down and spun around, realizing they were still surrounded. He reached down and scooped up his mask in one hand, holding it, the inside of it facing out. Dusting off his mask, he turned to face her.

Madness crept into her eyes, and excitement seemed to course through her legs up her torso as she asked, "Do any of you know what a sucking chest wound sounds like?" After she received her response of laughter from the soldiers, she continued, "It's when you stab someone between the second and third rib and they drown on their own fucking blood—"

The wind swept through the scene, carrying dust and sand across the cliffs and back down over the standoff below. Trees shifted as tendrils of leaves rustled and branches clicked like castanets, sending their noise up into the air. Parts of the old collapsed motel creaked. Waves crashed on the beach below, their melodic tones echoing rhythms that sounded reminiscent of a heartbeat. Birds chirped to life all at once, and the sun broke across the horizon behind the motel. A beat arrived with the rhythm; it danced as ethereal notes carried a direction past the soldiers' laughing forms, past the bloodied and bruised friends, past the enraged general's tiny form, and up to then over the cliff. It carried a tune many had danced to over the years but few ever heard.

Mason heard it. In an instant he spun, letting the mask leave his hands. Sand sprayed out in a semicircle around his form as his feet dug in and his body turned and angled.

The mask was falling and spinning toward the ground as his second step planted on cue with the beat he heard. The pop and hiss of gunfire echoed around him as the soldiers nearest the house opened fire on him. The gunfire inadvertently played into the rhythm. Mason was too lost in the beat to notice the bullets whizzing past as his third step landed.

His mask fell into the sand, sending grains of sand cascading around it, dusting the air as it came to rest face up, revealing one lone blue musical note on a black background.

Mason's fourth step landed on the beat just as Mary Helen held up a fist, signaling the soldiers to stop firing.

Mary Helen watched in shock as Mason sprinted to the cliff and leapt off, vanishing out of sight toward the rocks and surf below.

All that could be heard was the gentle surf in the distance until Mary Helen finally let out a surprised noise while clearing her throat. She turned back around to face Donathan and Ashley, adding through laughter, "Your friend is a goddamned lunatic. I mean, all this effort, and he goes and offs himse—"

Soldiers gasped and armor clattered as a large, dark form jolted up over the cliff and into the air. Mary Helen spun around on her heels to see the cause of the commotion as Mason came tumbling back down in the sand not far from his mask with a look of shock on his face. The ground shook with force, and dust filled the air, creating a natural smoke screen. Mary Helen held a hand over her face, trying to peer through it all.

The dust drifted thin enough that Barbie could be seen wearing jeans and a white tank top, perched up on top of the pink form of Beauty, who was still holding aloft the same body-armored soldier from the festival. Barbie had a condescending look on her face as she stared down toward Mary Helen. "Welcome to your nightmare, bitch."

"Open fire!" Mary Helen shouted, and the soldiers around her became galvanized, raising their rifles and taking shots. Rounds ricocheted in different directions off of Beauty's carapace as Barbie rolled back and behind the Shat.

During the confusion, Mason and Ashley had already scrambled to pick up their mask and bat and managed to sprint behind the Shat. Donathan paused a moment to surge, punch one of the soldiers in the face, and grab Mason's gun and backpack before coming to a jolting halt behind Beauty. Mason took his items out of Donathan's arms.

"Good timing," Ashley shouted over the gunfire toward Barbie. "I'm guessing Nyla signaled you?"

"Us, you mean?" Barbie replied.

Ashley clarified. "Yeah, you and Beauty."

"No." Barbie shook her head and peered out from behind one of Beauty's legs before pointing. "Us!"

The trio all leaned out behind her hesitantly.

The scene before them was chaos incarnate. A throng of soldiers huddled together and were firing off toward the side of the house, trying to stop something from advancing. Other soldiers seemed to be sprinting away in anticipation of something.

After a moment, a red Shat, whose armor seemed more bulbous and did not have a body dangling in front of it, came charging through the soldiers, sending them flying. As its body smashed through the rag dolls, it spun around in the sand while still sliding. For a moment, its legs tensed, then it playfully galloped in another direction, smashing into another group of soldiers with its large armor-clad head. It paused to send a bass scream up to the sky, which Beauty echoed. Then a shriller scream shot up from the distance.

A squad of soldiers sprinted around the house in a line and raised their rifles toward the red Shat.

A green blur fell out of the sky right behind them and in one swift motion separated their torsos from their legs, sending crimson spray up into the air. Behind them, a green Shat held one long, thin, sharp green leg up above itself. The rest of its spider-like legs were curled up as if poised to strike. Its head was smaller and buglike, its double jaw clicking in the morning sun as it cocked its head to one side, judging the scene before the rest of its legs pulsed to life and it skittered out of sight.

"Seems about time to go to work," Donathan said before holding up the sign for the number twenty. Ashley already had her headphones on and was mimicking Donathan's sign. Mason nodded and scrambled for his headphones before holding his hand up to match the sign. When everyone was in sync, they all reached down and cued up a song labeled "Dessa – Bullpen".

As the beat of the song rushed in, Mason stepped out from behind Beauty, who was still comfortably blocking stray bullets. Bodies of soldiers lay strewn around the parking lot, but more still surged from the house and the field. With the gun still dangling from his hip, he threw two long bursts ahead of him, causing the soldiers in his line of sight to duck down.

Ashley came out next, sprinting past as Mason continued throwing rounds downrange. As the song played, her bat sang to life ahead of her. The first soldier to bring his head up lost his helmet. The second soldier that tried to stand up got a crushed ankle. The third soldier, who tried to crawl away, got the full force of an overhead swing. She threw her bat at the next soldier and sprinted full speed toward another soldier trying to aim at her, sliding in the sand and dust between his legs and reaching up to disarm him by yanking the buttstock of his rifle out of his hands. Spinning around, she fired two shots into the enemy, then threw the rifle through the air.

Donathan surged out from behind Beauty and snatched the rifle out of the air and very quickly sped ahead, pausing to fire off two short bursts at each enemy that appeared. At one point, Beauty skittered out of sight behind the house. After a few minutes, soldiers stopped rushing out from that direction. When they turned back toward the clearing, the song had ended, and they found Mary Helen standing there, sword drawn, with an icy stare that could have destroyed a world.

"You think it matters?" Mary Helen asked. "You think I even give a shit that I lose one battalion? We have all the power. California is ours, and with or without these soldiers, I'll see the end of you." Music was playing in the distance; a guitar and drums could just barely be heard. Mary Helen continued, "Have you ever cut a man from his tear duct to the back of his neck?" The music grew louder.

Ashley leaned toward Donathan while removing her headphones and asked, "Do you hear that?" Donathan nodded while tucking away his headphones.

"It's messy business, that." Mary Helen's rant continued. "Half a person's face sags, and there's blood and stained flesh. Even after it's sewn up, it never quite looks right, and—" The music had grown intensely loud. Mary Helen turned toward the dune and shouted, "What the fuck is that noise?" A red truck came flying over the sand dune and smashed into Mary Helen, sending her flying across the clearing.

Loud rock music belted out of two large speakers strapped into the back of the vehicle as it skidded to a halt in front of the trio. Princess Jae shouted from the cab, "Get in!" and Nyla shouted from the passenger seat, "We have to go! Jae lit a match!"

Before the trio could respond, Barbie shouted, "Help!"

Barbie was struggling to hold Mary Helen from behind, her arms wrapped around Mary Helen's, pinning them to her side. Mary Helen kept smashing her head backward, left and right. The three Shats all stood behind them. The green Shat's posture shifted as it refolded its body in on itself, keeping the two low, green mandibles forward and revealing its slightly larger gray mandible above the other two. The limbs flexed for a moment, then steadied. Jae shouted something at the trio, but they were already running toward Barbie. "She can't see it coming," Barbie shouted. "Hold her head steady!"

Mason grabbed Mary Helen's left side, and Ashley took the right. Donathan grabbed her head and with all his strength helped hold her head in place. The green Shat hissed and then lurched forward at the opportunity, stabbing its larger mandible directly into the back of her head. The jolt knocked almost everyone free except Barbie, who had already spun around to face Mary.

Three sharp slaps crossed Mary Helen's face. "Fucking give up!" Barbie screamed at her. "It's over, bitch! We've beaten you!" Mary Helen's eyes twitched in random directions, her limbs flailed, and strength slowly seemed to drain from them.

"F-f-fuck you," Mary Helen groaned, and Barbie slapped her one more time until suddenly her eyes narrowed and a hiss issued forth out of her mouth.

Barbie's hand reached up and caressed Mary Helen's chin as she announced, "Hello, Gorgeous."

"We have to go now!" Princess Jae screamed.

The sound of an explosion ripped through Half Moon Bay.

24.

Skyline Boulevard

Zombie Civil Rights Group

Present Day

A SECOND EXPLOSION DETONATED, sending debris from the house flying through the air. "Okay, we're all in," Ashley shouted and slapped the top of the truck while leaning past the two large speakers mounted up against the cab.

"You two just run anywhere out of here," Barbie shouted, gesturing to the red and green Shats. They both roared one last time then leapt ahead down the road and began sprinting, the green Shat still dragging the flailing and semi-lifeless body of Mary Helen along with it. The red truck rumbled to life and aligned itself toward the same road, which led through the center of town.

Barbie climbed up on top of Beauty and said, "Ditch the weight!" Beauty rocked her large, pink head to one side and lofted the soldier's armored body away, leaving him sitting in a pile of his comrades' bloodied bodies. Then the Shat turned, and its legs spun to life like a freight train as it galloped down the road after the red truck.

After a moment the soldier stirred. "Hey guys, I had the weirdest dream. Guys?" The soldier glanced around the pile of bodies and quietly asked again, "Guys?"

The third bomb detonated, sending fire and destruction tearing through the parking lot and leaving a blackened crater.

The trio had settled down in the truck. More soldiers came into view around one of the corners, rushing toward the cliff they were fleeing. Princess Jae just angled the vehicle's build toward them, darting quickly to the other side of the road, and cackled as they scattered out of the way. Mason hunkered down on the left side, Donathan on the right, and Ashley was standing, holding onto the oversized speakers and looking back over her shoulder, trying to get eyes on Barbie. Princess Jae shouted back to the occupants, "I see you met the Queen of Crazytown."

"The Protectorate Army chick?" Shock bled into Donathan's voice.

Princess Jae took her eyes off the road just long enough to look back and reply, "She's my cousin."

"*Cousin?*" the trio of friends echoed and then scrambled to hold on as the truck turned to skid around a bend.

"Yeah... I can't stand her, though." Princess Jae laughed before saying, "I hit her with a train once."

Ashley mouthed the word, "Train?" to Donathan, who just shrugged.

A few more explosions trailed their egress out of Half Moon Bay. Finally, as they rounded the bend by the original science enclave, Ashley jammed a determined hand out, pointing behind the truck. Off in the distance, Beauty was sprinting through the rubble, her oversized, spindly legs a rush of motion as she navigated the road and rubble quickly being created by surrounding explosions. Occasional leaps caused her and Barbie to blur out of sight and up into the air momentarily. Ashley looked dumbfounded, then turned back around, slapping the speakers. "Mason, hold my shirt back here?" she asked and then leaned out over the side of the truck until she could see inside Princess Jae's window. "Does this thing have an mp3 player hookup?"

Princess Jae looked shocked to find Ashley's face leaning in the window. The vehicle jolted over a bump, then Jae leaned forward. Nyla could be seen in the passenger seat staring intently at a tablet computer. Jae sat back up and held up a fistful of wires and connectors toward Ashley and asked, "What kind?"

Ash managed to reach back and grab her mp3 player, scroll down to a song labeled "P.O.S. – Stand Up (Let's get murdered)," then hand the mp3 player into the cab. She clambered back to her feet behind the speakers and spun around to watch Beauty's sprint while shouting, "C'mon, girl!" At this point, the boys had stood up next to Ashley, so all three were cheering and waving their arms as the truck lumbered ahead over the old two-lane road through the cypress trees. Explosions were coming faster, and the road behind Barbie had vanished in a large fireball that seemed to be steadily moving closer. Debris shot over and past the truck.

Beauty's gallops slowed to match the beat of the song, keeping her just ahead of the flames until at one point the downbeat faded in, and Beauty slipped back into the inferno, both she and Barbie disappearing out of sight.

Ashley gasped as it happened, and the rest of the truck fell silent aside from the rumbling engine and sporadically skidding tires.

When the beat faded back up, Beauty leapt back out of the eye of the firestorm with Barbie still perched on top, leaning back a bit, seated comfortably with one leg curled up and the other on its side. Barbie took a moment to pat Beauty and smile as Ashley held both arms up, cheering as Mason and Donathan scrambled to hold her in the cab.

A close explosion belted forth on the far side of the road, and Jae banked the vehicle hard to avoid rubble from the blast. Beauty lunged up and over the projectiles. Another quaking explosion detonated just to their left, ripping a large tree in half and sending the severed trunk between Beauty and the truck. Barbie popped up to a sitting position as the shockwave hit but still held where she was until the mass of the trunk blocked her view. As the Shat cut sideways to go around the splintering and flaming branches, Barbie flexed her legs and bounded up and out of the seat. In two short steps, her bare feet sprinted across the mid-air tree trunk and spring-boarded off the thin end, landing in the back of the truck. Hands reached out to make sure she held her balance, but she shooed them off and climbed up over the cab of the vehicle as it vaulted and ricocheted around the volatile road. After making it over the cab, she hurdled back off the front of the pickup as Beauty skittered back into view, catching Barbie on its armored pink figure and darting out of the way of the truck. Once alongside the vehicle, the Shat matched its speed perfectly.

"Problem ahead," Nyla chimed in. "We're not going to make it. The last few bombs will detonate as we get there."

"Towards or away?" Jae shouted over the roar of explosions and engines.

"Uhh…" Nyla was fidgeting with the tablet.

Princess Jae asked again in a more determined tone, "Nyla, is the bridge going to collapse towards or away from us?"

"TOWARDS! *TOWARDS US!*" Nyla shouted.

The trio was still sitting in the back of the truck, Ashley and Donathan peering ahead over the top of the cab as the vehicle navigated the maze of animated rubble that spilled forth, sending rocks, trees, and concrete chunks across their path. The crack of an explosion close to the vehicle made everything shift, and Mason felt himself falling backward out of the truck. One of Donathan's hands lunged forward and grabbed the collar of Mason's ballistic vest, setting him back in the vehicle. Donathan smiled and said, "Hold on."

But Mason wasn't holding on, and he wasn't making eye contact with Donathan. During the explosion, he had seen a flaming chunk of rock flying directly from the other side of the road toward his face. Just before the vehicle shifted and he fell back, he had seen strange characters and a red mist appear in a flash, surround the rock, and then jolt it out of existence. In its place had appeared two doves that flew off in an arc away from the truck.

"Did you…?" Mason asked. Donathan smiled even more widely at Mason and patted him on the chest before looking away.

Ahead of the vehicle, bombs detonated just under the old highway bridge leading off Skyline Boulevard toward the ancient 280 freeway. The mass of concrete folded up and toward them as chunks shifted and fell. Flames licked from below the structure.

Donathan's voice mimicked Nyla's as he whispered, "Goodness."

Princess Jae didn't miss a beat; she jerked the wheel hard to the left, causing the vehicle to enter a deep skid up the crumbling chunk of the bridge. Tires screeched as the vehicle sped toward the chasm that had been ripped in part of the bridge ahead. "Hang on!" she shouted over her shoulder, out the cab's window.

Donathan dragged Ashley and Mason down as low as they could get into the truck's bed as the vehicle left the concrete. They could all feel the pickup carrying itself up, the momentary weightlessness of a large object ripping itself free of gravity's hold. The seconds that ticked by seemed like frozen minutes hanging on the edge of eternity. Then the shadow of the large pink Shat clouded overhead, its mass floating into view, its legs lassoing around the truck, its carapace covering the bed of the vehicle entirely. One of the speakers fell forward, and darkness engulfed them all before the impact.

"...ake up." Ashley was shaking Mason with force in the back of the ripped-up red truck. Mason opened his eyes and gazed up slowly toward Donathan and Ashley. Donathan handed Mason his mask. Aside from the sound of metal scraping concrete, the world seemed peaceful. The sun was brighter.

"Where are we?" Mason asked.

"280 heading north," Ashley replied. "How's your head?"

Mason subconsciously reached up and ran a hand over a knot on the front of his forehead. "I'm not sure."

He paused to draw a breath, then added, "I've spent more time unconscious in the last day than awake."

Donathan's smile grew wide, warm, and genuine before he said, "You missed it. Beauty draped herself over us and held us in the cab as the vehicle smashed into the other side of the bridge. It was... an awesome sight to see. I don't know how they managed it. For a moment, I thought we were going to die falling, and then the next moment I thought we were going to be crushed."

Mason sat up and realized the bed of the truck was slanted. Ripped and jagged metal extended off the back and toward the asphalt, issuing sparks as it dragged along the freeway. "I can see that." Peering off to his side, Mason caught sight of Barbie perched comfortably on Beauty's form as they lumbered slowly forward, matching pace with the wrecked pickup. Barbie was staring ahead and enjoying puffs of a cigarette dangling out of her mouth.

"So what happens now?" Mason asked as the sun glared down on the disheveled vehicle and its occupants.

"Not exactly sure," Donathan replied. "Dad just said to find you all and Princess Jae. That was part one of the plan, and well..." He hesitated a moment and motioned toward the cab of the truck. "You saw that Jae doesn't seem to have the answers." Donathan looked disappointed as the last syllables faded away.

Ashley looked from Mason back toward Donathan and then ahead of the truck's path northward and said in a determined voice, "I guess we need a part two, then."

"And music." Donathan fumbled for the mp3 player still attached to the cord and dangling into the truck's bed.

"And music," Mason and Ashley agreed as the beat faded in.

Falling Sands

The Judge

Two weeks after the detonation of Half Moon Bay

THE WOOD-PANELED WALLS creaked as heat escaped them in the early dusk hours. Three individuals stood lined up, shoulder-to-shoulder in the office. A short pudgy man with large eyes and dark hair parted to the right wore a green t-shirt and dark slacks with black tennis shoes; he was slouching off to the right. In the center of the group, a woman stood tall, wearing a black Kangol Shavora Baker Cap. Long red hair flowed down past her shoulders, accentuated by her pale skin. Green lace lined the edges of her jet-black halter top and trailed off, draping over her matching dark slacks and tennis shoes. On her far side was a wild-eyed man with a shaved head and pale skin, wearing a brown-furred suit with dark stains pockmarked across it. Backpack straps were lashed over his shoulders and attached to a large-eyed mascot outfit with a brown furry head on his back. One of the furry's ears was folded down and flopped slightly as the man shifted from left to right nervously on the dusty wooden floor.

The Judge spun around in his wide desk chair, his belly protruding massively as he edged forward toward his desk. One of his pudgy hands fumbled across the desktop and found a file, which he shoved toward the center of the group. The woman stepped forward to accept it, gave it a cursory glance, and added, "We've already been briefed."

"Your Honor?" The Judge's snide faux-rich tone slid into the conversation with all the grace of a deadly asp in the dark of night. "Forgotten Protectorate standards already?"

"No...Your Honor," Nym replied through clenched teeth, holding up the file in front of her, "But we've read this already, and we know our targets pretty well."

"Yes, well..." The Judge paused to clear his throat and dragged another file closer, opening it up and spreading out the contents to reveal dossiers of the three individuals standing in front of him. The words "massive collateral damage" were written in red and stood out above every other sentence on the files. "I certainly didn't want to call in the Fine Line Protectorate on this, but it seems my general underestimated them"—The Judge paused to cast a stern glare at Nym—"as well."

An uncomfortable moment passed, and finally the Judge turned his gaze back to the dossiers. "Goblin, is it?"

A fake upper-class British accent that was a strange mix of comedy and drama issued forth from the man on the right as he tugged at the edge of his green shirt, looking down and refusing to make eye contact with the Judge, "Yes... Well, that's me, isn't it?" Goblin finally looked up to lock eyes with the Judge. "The Judge, is it?"

"Amusing." The Judge replied in a very dull tone. "And lastly we have... Crooks?" The fur-covered man nodded profusely. "Why is this man dressed like a stuffed animal?"

Crooks's face lit up with a wide smile, and he cocked a head to one side.

"Oh, Crooksy doesn't talk much," Nym added. "He's a mascot of sorts... Making a statement about the animal within."

The Judge leaned forward curiously and said, "But it says here in the file that you are 'Vampires.' So that would make him a bat without wings." The Judge's voice seemed amused to point this out. Crook's face soured a bit.

"Oh, we don't mention that..." Nym's smile flashed venomously for a moment, her eyes narrowing and her smile widening. "Your Honor."

The Judge sat back, sensing the tension between him and the group. "Perhaps a demonstration is in order," he proclaimed while reaching for the old-style microphone on the far edge of his desk. "Coadjutant. CO-AD-JU-TANT." His voice boomed over the loudspeakers.

A sunburned man with a receding hairline and a sharp smile stuck his head around the corner and into the room. "Yes, Judge?"

"BRING ME AN OLDER...OH—" The Judge's voice had continued to boom through the microphone. He took his hand off the button at the base of the microphone before continuing, "Bring me an older slave from one of the pens. Someone who won't be missed much from the day's work."

The balding man nodded and left, and running footsteps echoed from the hallway. The Judge sat up taller and just stared at the three members of the Fine Line Protectorate, who returned his gaze. Minutes passed. Crooks shifted uncomfortably every so often and looked away. A sly smile drifted across Nym's lips. Goblin refused to blink.

Finally, the echo of footfalls cascaded into the room as an older man wearing yellow jumper leggings and a torn white shirt, tinted from dust, was shoved in the room. A tuft of white hair sat up on his scalp. His skin was leathery, and a ratty, dirty white beard hung forward and off of his chin. The old man made quiet noises of shock as a body-armor-clad guard shoved him through the line of individuals until he was standing directly in front of the Judge's desk. The Judge slowly nodded, and the guard turned and exited the room.

The old man's shoulders were hunched forward. The man seemed uncomfortable from standing, and his eyes were full of fear as he avoided eye contact with the Judge.

"Proceed," the Judge commanded.

Nym gave a frustrated look over one shoulder to Goblin and then back over her other toward Crooks, "Well it's not exactly Cheesecake Factory, is it?" she said as she stepped forward and turned the old man around so he had his back to the Judge. "Are you afraid of the dark, old man?"

The man just shook his head meekly, and Nym lunged forward, wrapping both her hands around it and holding it tightly in place, her mouth right next to his ear as she whispered sinisterly, "Why not?"

All at once, Goblin and Crooks dashed forward, grabbing the old man. Crooks's fur-covered hands pulled, and Goblin's matched his force in the opposite direction. Nym locked dark eyes with the Judge as the old man screamed. A moment later, the arm Goblin was yanking severed itself at the shoulder, and arterial spray filled the room, covering Goblin first and then showering up toward Nym's face as she spun on her heel, throwing the body of the man behind her. Goblin and Crooks launched themselves onto the twitching torso, and Nym turned back to face the Judge with lost eyes and a malicious grin on her face, cackling slightly to herself as she gasped to catch her breath.

The Judge burst forth with tiny, sharp applause, his large rotund hands repeatedly forcing precise little clapping motions. Overflowing with a fit of laughter, he kicked and thrashed in his chair a moment. "Oh, wonderful! What a show! I... Clearly, you do have many talents." Nym's bloodied face was vacant-eyed, staring straight ahead, her smile vanished. Amusement drained from the Judge's face as he noticed a few drops of blood had spilled onto the front end of his desk. His sneer turned to frustration but was shrugged away as he reached down and fumbled through one of his desk drawers.

"When you find my young general, would you be so kind as to place this on her?" the Judge asked as he held a closed fist over the top of his desk. Nym's eyes refocused and turned toward the Judge's hand. A devilish smile edged back across her face as she held up a bloody hand and leaned forward, opening a palm under the Judge's fist and dripping more blood onto his desktop. The Judge swallowed hard and made an annoyed sound before opening his palm and letting a round object fall into Nym's grasp. "Now, drag that mess into the hallway and send my coadjutant in with a mop."

The night was choking, suffocating the sky as footfalls trampled long grass and fallen branches. The forest was a symphony of screeches and broken twigs screaming out his location. The cold air felt acidic as its sharp taste jabbed its way into his lungs. Muscles ached as he ran on rolled ankles and popping knees. The palms of one of his hands had been bleeding from where he had fallen, tripping over one of the low tombstones hidden in the unkempt cemetery he had stumbled into. Looking back over his shoulder only revealed more darkness. Just beyond his vision, the dark forest appeared blotchy and warped, giving the illusion that something was standing just out of his view, or maybe it actually was. He had run on and off for an hour, and that only seemed to bring the hungry shrieks closer, only seemed to add more desperation to the chase. He could hear the snapping of their jaws as they closed the trap around him.

Panicking, Carl cast his eyes about the cemetery, looking for shelter. "Why did we have to push sunset?" Carl thought frantically as he sprinted toward a mausoleum near the center of the graveyard. Its old cement roof was weathered, the edges dull and rounded. Another screech ripped through the night nearby, and Carl threw his entire weight into the large metal door. The round ring handle clunked against the iron as he did. The large door withstood every blow. The shrieks around Carl grew sharper as if they, along with the door, were taunting his failure.

Dark, violent fog issued up from an old sunken grave next to the mausoleum. Carl continued to scrape at the door with fear and frustration, not noticing the bald old man behind him, crawling up out of the grave, his right hand doing most of the work, then standing up and shivering clay and dirt off an old gray suit with a tattered white open-collared shirt underneath. The skinny, short man produced a meat cleaver that had been hanging, tied to one of his hips, and stepped forward up onto a step behind Carl, who was still clawing at the door. The purple mist hung in the air around the bald man, who sniffed loudly.

Carl froze, and all the noise of flesh on metal halted. The screeching also seemed to die down suddenly. Slowly and forced, Carl managed to tiptoe around in a semicircle to face the round-domed, wide-eyed man.

A large scar crossed the man's face, his large sharp nose and skinny form angled up at Carl, both hands held behind his back in a non-threatening pose.

"H-h-hello?" Carl whined and then slowly held out a hand.

The elderly man sniffed the air again and looked confused at Carl's hand and then motioned over his shoulder toward the grave he had just crawled out of. "Any idea why I crawled in there?" the old man asked in a high-pitched voice of curiosity.

Carl looked confused and stood frozen, his arm still held out offering a handshake. "I uh...well...that is...I don't... know?" The inflection of his last word rose in fear.

The old man lowered his gaze on Carl, licked his lips, and then smiled, tilting his head to one side. "Well then..." His smile became warm, and he giggled. The giggles turned into laugher. Carl nervously mimicked his laughter. The senior man's laughter became a fit of whoops broken up with sharply slanting smiles that flashed across his face as he motioned toward the door of the mausoleum. "How about a hand, then?"

Carl nodded and began to lower his hand down toward his side. A flash and a jolt shot through Carl, causing him to raise a gushing stump toward his face as it sprayed forth blood. Sharp pain set in as his breath left him and shock flooded into its place. "Wh-Wh-Whuh." Looking up, he saw the very pleased old man restrapping the butcher knife to his hip and pausing to pick up Carl's hand off the cement step. The purple fog swarmed around him, and then the mist itself seemed to flex and fade as the old man stepped off the slab step and held Carl's hand up to his own left wrist. The elderly man leaned back, sucking at his teeth a moment, and held his new hand aloft, flexing it into motion in the moonlight before adding, "I think 'Razorwrist' is appropriate." When satisfied, he turned back to the Ravens that had frozen in a semicircle around the graves, their arms pulled in tight, wrists angled down sharply, their heads all cocking and twitching in different directions as if judging the situation.

Razorwrist noticed them all at once and strutted out toward them, announcing, "Oh ho ho! A procession... look at what we've become." His arms stretched out wide, palms up, the fingertips of his new hand wiggling in the night.

Carl managed to choke out a scream, and all the Ravens screeched and leapt past Razorwrist, their teeth clacking and gnashing as they descended upon the bloodied, struggling man.

Razorwrist turned to watch their attack. Then, shrugging, he turned away, tucking his hands in his pockets, stopping suddenly to pull clay out of one of them, and leaned forward to study the falling particles drifting off the palm of his hand. "Well, then. I suppose the ceremony is over," he said nonchalantly.

Shaking the remaining clay off his hand, Razorwrist paused to dust off one of his shoulders and turned to look up toward the moon and announce in a determined voice, "Let's *punch* the clock."

Falkor Publishing is a tiny little sci-fi book imprint based in Tulsa, OK. We're the child of Auryn Creative and we're pretty excited to be working with some amazing new authors like Steven Mix, Joanne Johnson, and Steve Shumaker as well as editors, artists, designers, and creatives of all kinds.

We want to especially thank Jennifer M., Karen L., and Joe C. for believing and supporting.

We hope you get to love our writers and artists as much as we do. To keep up with what's going on at Falkor, visit falkorpublishing.com

For news and updates about Goodbye from the Edge of Never (including updates about the next book), visit stevenmix.com

We're pretty darn happy about what all we've been up to lately, and we hope you keep in touch. Thanks!

CPSIA information can be obtained
at www.ICGtesting.com
Printed in the USA
FFOW03n0051180814
6827FF